*A Candlelight
Ecstasy Romance®*

**"ARE YOU SO MONEY HUNGRY THAT YOU
MARRIED A MAN YOU DIDN'T LOVE?" MITCH
DEMANDED.**

"I don't like the way you said that," Jackie replied
angrily.

"Is there another way of putting it? Didn't your
mother ever tell you that money makes a cold lover?"

Pride brought Jackie to her feet. "My mother was too
busy trying to raise three kids on her own—she didn't
have time for talking. And my father was too busy chasing women to spend time with his family. A man after
your own heart, I'm sure."

"What makes you think that? I'm really a simple man.
You're the one who's complicated, Jackie. I wonder if
you even know who you are."

Jackie looked at him coldly. "I'm an enchantress,
that's what I am." She turned away to hide her tears.

CANDLELIGHT ECSTASY CLASSIC ROMANCES

CANDLELIGHT ECSTASY ROMANCES®

QUANTITY SALES

Most Dell Books are available at special quantity discounts when purchased in bulk by corporations, organizations, and special-interest groups. Custom imprinting or excerpting can also be done to fit special needs. For details write: Dell Publishing Co., Inc., 1 Dag Hammarskjold Plaza, New York, NY 10017, Attn.: Special Sales Dept., or phone: (212) 605-3319.

INDIVIDUAL SALES

Are there any Dell Books you want but cannot find in your local stores? If so, you can order them directly from us. You can get any Dell book in print. Simply include the book's title, author, and ISBN number, if you have it, along with a check or money order (no cash can be accepted) for the full retail price plus 75¢ per copy to cover shipping and handling. Mail to: Dell Readers Service, Dept. FM, 6 Regent Street, Livingston, N.J. 07039.

KNIGHT OF ILLUSIONS

Jane Atkin

A CANDLELIGHT ECSTASY ROMANCE®

Published by
Dell Publishing Co., Inc.
1 Dag Hammarskjold Plaza
New York, New York 10017

Dell ® TM 681510, Dell Publishing Co., Inc.

Candlelight Ecstasy Romance®, 1,203,540, is a registered trademark of Dell Publishing Co., Inc., New York, New York.

ISBN: 0-440-14596-1

Printed in the United States of America

April 1987

10 9 8 7 6 5 4 3 2 1

WFH

To Our Readers:

We have been delighted with your enthusiastic response to Candlelight Ecstasy Romances®, and we thank you for the interest you have shown in this exciting series.

In the upcoming months we will continue to present the distinctive sensuous love stories you have come to expect only from Ecstasy. We look forward to bringing you many more books from your favorite authors and also the very finest work from new authors of contemporary romantic fiction.

As always, we are striving to present the unique, absorbing love stories that you enjoy most—books that are more than ordinary romance. Your suggestions and comments are always welcome. Please write to us at the address below.

Sincerely,

The Editors
Candlelight Romances
1 Dag Hammarskjold Plaza
New York, New York 10017

To my husband, with love

KNIGHT OF ILLUSIONS

CHAPTER ONE

Mitch opened one blue eye, closed it, then opened the other. He could see Carly standing above him holding her watering can, wet plants dripping all around him. It probably didn't say much for his reflexes that it took him a while to realize he wasn't alone.

"Did you get thrown out of your apartment or do you just enjoy punishing your body?" Carly O'Neill bantered, looking down at her boss. Mitch Corey was laying prone on his office couch where she assumed he'd spent the night.

"Don't you be bright with me this morning," he sneered, parrying.

"Sorry." Carly grinned. "I don't know how I could have forgotten, after working for you for three years now, that you don't come alive until noon."

"I don't think Mickey Spillane has to put up with all this back talk from his secretary." Mitch groaned, swinging his long, tightly muscled legs off the side arm of the couch where they'd been perched for the last three hours. He sat up trying not to feel the crink of pain in his back. Mind over matter wasn't any help.

"Mickey Spillane is probably too busy to notice," Carly answered, needling some more as she set the watering can on the edge of Mitch's desk. She made sure to place it on yesterday's newspaper to avoid leaving a water ring. Not that it would have mattered much. Mitch had bought all the office furniture second hand when he'd first opened his private investigating office five and a half years ago. It all already had the look of used and abused. Mitch had told her that he'd chosen his particular selection of office furniture as an intentional psychological ploy to engender credibility. A prospective client doesn't hire a private eye who looks brand new. The truth, and he knew that she knew it, was that when he'd opened his office after leaving the LAPD he hadn't had much more than two nickels to rub together. He had done a great deal better for himself since then and he was well on his way to building a reputation as the best private investigator in town. Carly knew Mitch Corey's success was as much a result of skill as it was determination. Being successful was as vital to him as breathing.

"Are you saying that you don't have enough to do around here to earn that nice paycheck I hand you every week?" Mitch asked kiddingly. He rotated his head trying to get the kink out of his neck.

"Do you hear me saying that? I don't hear me saying that." Carly laughed softly and then sat down on the couch. She massaged Mitch's shoulders with a lot more strength than one would have expected from a petite brunette. "Now are you ready for a lecture? I don't want to hit you when you're already down."

Mitch gyrated his broad shoulders to the feel of Carly's hands. "I'm as ready as I'm going to be today. Lecture away."

Carly pounded a little harder than necessary.

"Mitch Corey, here you are with the biggest case that's come into this office and my guess is that you spent the whole night philandering and muddling your brain."

Mitch laughed. It hurt his head. To the best of his recollection he hadn't had more than an hour's sleep. "Yesterday was Wednesday. You've been my secretary long enough to know that I never philander on Wednesdays."

"Don't tell me Captain Scotto of the Los Angeles Police Department wore you out so much that you couldn't have crawled home. When I left you here last night at seven you did say that you were going over to the precinct to nose around." Carly dealt out some more hard shots across Mitch's back.

"Easy, honey," Mitch complained, emitting a groan, but not moving out of the way of Carly's busy hands. "I did go over to the precinct where I spent all last night and the better part of the morning while you were curled up into a blissful ball on your bed."

"I sleep on my back, straight out, for your information," Carly retorted.

"Care to offer me the chance to verify that?" Mitch asked, coating his voice with mock innuendo.

Carly pushed at Mitch's shoulders, turning him to face her. "Are you working yourself up to tell me something important to the case or are you just trying to work yourself up?"

Mitch winked and ran his fingers through his unruly light-brown hair. He could feel that he was way overdue for a trim. "All you have to do is say the right word, darling. It wouldn't take much for me to work myself up for you."

"I've got more than one word for you. I've got a whole sentence," Carly said through an imitation of a frown while she adjusted the ends of Mitch's navy blue silk tie. She fit the knot back up tight to his neck.

Mitch took Carly's hands away and loosened his tie again. "What sentence is that, pray tell?"

"You have to dictate a report to me today for the insurance group that hired you to find out who's the new fence here in Tinseltown. Do you have anything for me to fill in between periods and commas?"

"I'm not talking on an empty stomach," Mitch countered, giving the impression that he always gave and that was that he took everything light and easy. It wasn't true. There was a very hard core to Mitch Corey.

"I'm going to compromise myself just this one time and make you a pot of coffee. I'll even order up some breakfast to go along with it, if you promise not to let the word out." Carly stood up and smiled down into the very blue eyes of Mitch Corey. "What would you like? And that's not to be misconstrued as a leading question."

"Too bad. I thought I was starting to get lucky and you were getting tired of that new fellow of yours," Mitch returned.

"From what I hear you get lucky too often for your own good," Carly retorted. "Now one more time, what would you like for breakfast?"

"I'd like two aspirins and a Screwdriver to wash them down," Mitch answered, watching Carly make a face. "On second thought," he added, "I can live without the orange juice. Just get me the driver." Mitch stretched his leg and felt around in his trouser pocket.

He took out a pack of crushed Marlboros and lit one up. He got in one long drag before Carly took the cigarette out of his mouth.

"You quit . . . Remember?" Carly admonished, dropping the cigarette into a half-empty container of yesterday's black coffee.

"You know me. I've got a brain like a sieve." He didn't bother to light up another one. The first one had tasted like straw. He had quit two months ago.

"I hope you're not planning to take this act on the road," Carly answered as she sat down in the chair behind Mitch's desk. She picked up the phone and ordered eggs over easy and bacon for both of them from the coffee shop in the lobby. "While we're waiting you can start talking," she said, hanging up the phone with a flourish. "Did you pick up anything last night at the precinct?"

"Nothing that was catching, I hope . . ." Mitch got up from the couch and walked some circulation back into his legs. "I must say that Scotto, as usual, was thrilled to see me. He sat through all my snappy dialogue as catatonic as ever. He wouldn't even give me the satisfaction of blinking an eye."

"What else?"

"What else? I went over to the robbery division to chew the fat with some of the boys. There wasn't much left to chew. Scotto had already chewed off most of their heads."

"Who can blame him with the rash of jewelry robberies that have been going on in the last ten months?"

"What's bothering the department and the insurance companies even more is that none of the jewelry that's been heisted is surfacing, not even rearranged.

15

According to the actuary tables that the insurance companies keep, a percentage of stolen jewelry is almost always recovered even after the claims are met."

"As you said, the insurance boys don't appreciate it when their actuary tables don't jive."

"Right." Mitch grinned at Carly's imitation of his speech. "But I still posted a vote of sympathy for my old friends in blue. Like me, they don't figure some fence to be just sitting on all the stuff. There has got to be a way they're moving it because there's no profit if hot rocks sit in a warehouse. Between you and me, I'm still of the opinion that it's being marketed outside of LA and not a piece at a time. Whoever is doing the marketing has got themselves a nice sophisticated operation."

"Opinion noted." Carly smiled. "Is that it for last night?"

"Not quite." Mitch's features tightened. "A call came through, another house in Beverly Hills had been broken into, which made it the second this week. But this one had a twist."

"What twist?"

"A patrol car had been passing by. A new kid, fresh from the academy, zipped out of the car and bip-e-de-bop he nailed one of a trio making their exits. The two that got away had the jewelry, keeping our ever-loving fence in business."

"Since you sometimes lose me with your lingo, does 'bip-e-de-bop' mean that one of them was killed?"

"Yeah, but not right off." Mitch stopped moving to gaze out of his office window. "Anyway, the boys from the precinct went out and I song and danced my way into tagging along. To make a short story shorter, the one that didn't get away was Johnny Marks."

"Johnny Marks . . . Wait a minute. Isn't Johnny Marks the guy you gave character testimony for about a year ago when he was charged with selling stripped parts from stolen cars?"

"Now I know why I pay you so well. You have a fantastic memory," Mitch said, managing a light tone. But he'd had to fight for it. "Did I ever mention that I had played in the same group with Johnny Marks, many moons ago, when he and I planned on being musicians?" Mitch thought he heard Carly's quiet "yes." He wasn't really paying attention or really seeing anything, though he continued to stare out the window. He was thinking about Johnny Marks and remembering how young and eager he'd been back then with his lifetime full of plans. Mitch had had some other kinds of lifetime plans himself back then.

"Was Johnny Marks dead when you got there?" Carly asked somberly. She came around from behind Mitch's desk.

"He was hanging on by a slim thread and losing the battle." Mitch sat down in the chair Carly had just vacated.

"I bet that didn't stop you from asking him a few questions." Carly's remark was not meant to be derisive and she could see that Mitch understood. He had a job to do and he always did it well. The job required that emotions take second place.

"You're starting to sound a little cynical there, Carly O'Neill. Must be the company you're keeping from nine to five. Or whatever the hours are that you're here."

"What did Johnny Marks tell you?" Carly persisted, going about it quietly. She recognized that Mitch was only making a half-hearted attempt to kid around. He was upset, but she knew he'd deny it if she asked.

Mitch sighed. "Johnny always did prefer to wisecrack. He wisecracked his way to the end. His last words for me were, 'Have a fantasy.' A little original, don't you think? He could have just told me to go take a hike."

Carly watched Mitch open the deep side drawer of his desk and take out the worn leather case that held his saxophone. She knew him well enough to know that he intended to be melancholy for a while.

"I'll let you know when breakfast arrives," Carly said softly, as she walked to Mitch's office door. She also knew that Mitch took his depression alone.

"Here's to fantasies, Johnny . . . yours and mine," Mitch whispered to himself as he fixed the mouthpiece on his horn.

Jacqueline Lacey reclined in her tub and responded dreamily to the feel of a mountain of warm fragrant bubbles. Her long honey-blond hair was wrapped up in a towel. She had an hour to spare before she had to get dressed and truly become Jacqueline Lacey. Just yesterday she had been Marie Antoinette attired in opulent gem-laden splendor. It wasn't always easy to leave the fantasy behind and make the adjustment back into the real world. Jacqueline closed her green eyes wanting to hold on to the fantasy for just a little longer. But just as she was getting away, the harsh steady ring of her doorbell drew her annoyingly back.

"Coming . . . I'm coming," Jackie called out, wrapping a large terry robe around her wet body.

She opened her apartment door to Alex Shaffner, her business partner, who stood tall and rangy with his finger still poised on the bell. Jackie smiled a welcome. "You couldn't wait to hear all the details, right?"

"Right." Alex smiled back as he stepped in. "I also figured I'd save a few bucks and let you make me breakfast."

"Let me guess . . . Laurie must be sleeping late?" Jackie kidded.

"I insisted. She was up half the night with the baby."

"I don't know how Laurie puts up with having a baby and a grown infant to take care of as well."

Alex laughed. "Look who's calling who a grown infant—Miss Make Believe Fantasy herself!"

" 'Ms.' Make Believe Fantasy," Jackie corrected teasingly as she unwound the towel from around her head. Her thick blond hair tumbled down almost to the small of her back.

"Well, 'Ms.' Make Believe Fantasy, I'm sure happy to see you. I worry about you when you're away. I've been thinking that we should really start to check out the people we book on these fantasy vacations of yours before you go and hide yourself away for ten days at a time."

"Do I hear the sound of dragging feet? This scheme of mine is starting to make us a lot of money. Stop worrying." Jackie slipped her hand under Alex's arm.

"We're making a lot of money, but that still doesn't stop me from worrying." Alex frowned.

19

"I've been fending for myself since I was eighteen and that gives me ten years of practice. Anyway, I enjoy a little risk taking. I get cranky when I'm bored." Jackie flashed a captivating smile that was intended to allay any of her partner's concern. "Now if you want breakfast I'll open up a box of cornflakes for you. That's about as domestic as I get."

"Which brings up another point," Alex said, following Jackie into her kitchen.

"What point?" Jackie asked over her shoulder as she fished around in a pantry cabinet that contained more of an accumulation of uneatable odds and ends than food.

"Your personal life." Alex parked himself on a stool in front of a butcher block counter.

Jackie walked out of the pantry victoriously holding a box of cornflakes. "What about my personal life?"

"Laurie and I were talking," Alex began and would have continued if Jackie hadn't cut him off.

"Whenever you start off with, 'Laurie and I were talking' you wind up by telling me that what I need, besides money, is some man in my life. Well, I don't." Jackie poured the cornflakes in a bowl and handed it to him.

"I'm still willing to bet that one of these days some guy is going to come along and sweep you off your feet."

Jackie walked to her refrigerator and got out a container of milk. "You would bet on anything, Alex, no matter what the odds."

"You know what I think the problem is?" Alex said.

"Is this a new problem or the same one?" Jackie asked, starting to get irritated.

"The problem is that you intimidate men," Alex went on, unperturbed.

"Just how do I do that?"

"You're too independent and self-assured. You have to learn to lean a little."

Alex didn't know it but Jackie had already tried that once and found that she didn't have to lean on a man at all—not for financial security and especially not for love. Only a fool depends on love. She'd learned early on that love came with a built-in timetable—a clock that always ran out. "I prefer to fill my head with fantasies and line both of our pockets with gold. And all I want to hear from you, after I get dressed, is whether you've booked a full house for King Arthur's Round Table."

"That is problem number two," Alex said as Jackie started out of the kitchen.

Jackie made an aboutface, pulled out a chair and sat down.

The travel agency office of Have a Fantasy Vacation was not all that far from Mitch Corey's own office, which was in a high rise further north on Wilshire Boulevard. As Mitch stepped in through a double set of glass doors on street level, he wondered at the many times he'd passed by this place without noticing it. He wondered, too, if he'd finally popped his cork. It was just too much of a long shot to even imagine that Johnny Marks's last dying words had any association to this travel agency. But after a week of nothing, Mitch was willing to explore any long shot no matter how long it was.

From a central counter wrapped in seamless plush

carpeting a young attractive female receptionist watched Mitch approach.

"Good morning," Shannon Grant said, smiling warmly when Mitch reached the counter and took off his dark sunglasses. "Can I help you?"

Mitch matched her smile and thought of a way or two before he got his mind back on business. "I'd like to see either Alex Shaffner or Jacqueline Lacey," he answered, before glancing around. There were five desks beyond the counter and they were all occupied. A unisex staff was either shuffling papers or busy on the phone. Mitch noted two private offices in the rear, jungles of plants and a couple of expensive-looking sofas prominently placed.

"Mr. Shaffner is out to lunch, but Ms. Lacey is in. Are you here to plan a fantasy vacation?" There was just enough of a come-on in her voice to be noticed.

Mitch's smile broadened. "I guess I'm obviously in the right place but I think I'm going to need a little more incentive before I can plan. Will you check if Ms. Lacey can see me?" He had already checked on the proprietorship. The place was managed under a two-party partnership. Alex Shaffner and Jacqueline Lacey divvied up the titles and profits between them. Mitch had a friend at the precinct checking for more stats.

Shannon spoke on an inter-office phone for a moment. Hanging up, she gave Mitch the high sign and pointed her finger for him to follow her. It led him to one of the rear offices. Gold blocked lettering proclaimed its occupant. Mitch gave the door a quick knock and then he stepped in.

The office was large and she was at the far end of

22

the room sitting behind a light wood desk that had been lacquered so high it might have picked up an image. The image it might have picked up caught Mitch by surprise. He'd formed a picture of Jacqueline Lacey in his mind. It was a kind of game that he played with himself. Give him a name and he made up a face. He'd figured Jacqueline Lacey to be in her mid-forties and attractive. She wasn't anywhere near her mid-forties . . . Late twenties, he guessed, and as far as being attractive, he hadn't figured hard enough. She was beautiful and that appraisal came from a man who appreciated women. Jacqueline Lacey was 99 percent class. The one percent leftover Mitch decided to leave debatable.

"Please have a seat," Jackie said, tracking Mitch's approach without any discernible emotion crossing her face. But Jacqueline Lacey was seeing what other women saw in Mitch Corey. There was no missing his kind of sexy virility even if he hadn't been over six feet tall. Jackie took in his blue eyes, his deep tan, and the ruggedness of his face. She even took in the dark sunglasses visible in the front pocket of his white sports jacket that was opened to expose a well-filled cranberry-colored knit shirt. She took all of him in and she disliked him immediately.

Mitch took a seat in front of her desk. There were two, each nicely padded in lavender suede, matching the chair that she was sitting on. A yellow linen jacket was draped over the back of hers.

"I'll be with you in just a moment," Jackie said, picking back up her 14-karat-gold-plated Cross pen and going back to work on a piece of paper.

"Take your time," Mitch said comfortably. He used

his to study her some more. He contemplated whether her blond hair was natural. He wondered how she would look with her hair loose. She had her hair pushed back into a tight French braid that defied any loose strands to escape. As far as he could tell she wore very little makeup. A light layer of mascara was about all Mitch could detect on lashes that circled the greenest pair of eyes he'd ever seen.

"I'm Jacqueline Lacey." Jackie stretched her hand out across her desk.

"I kind of figured that out by now," Mitch said, giving her a teasing grin. "I'm Mitch Corey." He took her hand and gave it a firm shake. At the count of three, she drew away.

Jackie ignored his attempt at humor. "We like to know what brought you to us. Was it a recommendation or one of our ads?" she asked professionally.

"One of your ads," Mitch replied.

"Newspaper, magazine, or TV?" Jackie pulled open her top desk drawer for a piece of blank paper.

"Which ad were you in?" Mitch stretched his legs out and crossed his ankles.

"I wasn't in any of them." She favored him with a cool stare.

Mitch eyed her back, looking amused. "The truth is I saw your sign outside and I just walked in. I hope you do handle off-the-street traffic?"

"I assume then that you're not familiar with any of our fantasy vacations," she said, tapping the top of her desk with the tip of her pen. Of all days, why had she picked today to skip lunch?

"You assume right," Mitch answered, giving her a smile. "But I think I am in the need of a fantasy and

I'm sure you can provide one that I'd enjoy." He baited her a little just for the hell of it, not really expecting a rise. He wondered what it took to shake her up. He also wondered what it took to warm her up.

"When do you expect to be taking your vacation? And how much time do you have off?" Jackie parlayed her questions one after the other without any pause. She was becoming quite irritated.

Mitch didn't know how far he wanted to go on just a hunch. Chances were that Jacqueline Lacey was legit and so was her business. But since he did have the ball, he decided he might as well run with it. "I'm free after next week and I can take off as much time as I like."

"Don't tell me . . ." Jackie said wryly. "You must be in between pictures."

Mitch's expression showed momentary surprise. "Where did you get that idea? I'm not an actor."

"Oh . . ." Jackie's expression showed some momentary surprise as well. She usually did pretty well at matching people to professions.

"I guess appearances can be deceiving." That was a point that he always kept in mind. "Now why don't you tell me about your fantasy vacations?"

Jackie battled an urge to tell Mitch Corey that all their fantasy vacations were booked up for the next twenty years. But her better business sense forced her to ignore the minor personal irritation he was causing. "We recreate a fantasy from out of the past and we provide the proper costuming, props, and setting to go along with it. We can offer you two weeks of sailing around the Caribbean as a pirate on a pirate's boat. Or an Antony and Cleopatra cruise down the Nile. And if you don't care to be on the water we have a number of . . ."

"You mentioned props. Just what do you mean?" Mitch interrupted her monologue.

"What exactly do you want to know?" Jackie had the feeling he was getting ready to pitch something from out of left field. She braced herself.

"For example, you did say a pirate's cruise and what came to mind was a picture of all that pirate's booty. Do you fill up trunks with gold doubloons and jewels?"

"Yes, but they're all fake. Everything is rented from the studios." People ask all sorts of questions.

Mitch thought she looked uncomfortable or she could have been just annoyed. He'd already surmised that she didn't particularly cotton to him. He speculated on what it was about him that she didn't like. His appearance and personality seemed to sum it up.

"We have a Tarzan and Jane safari in the jungles of Peru where you'll be looking for the lost City of Gold," Jackie went on. "That might interest you."

"Do you have an Arabian Night's fantasy? I wouldn't mind being a sheikh," Mitch teased, playing into her oblique sarcasm. He also gave his deductive abilities a spin. A pirate's trunk of supposedly fake gems was one sweetheart of a way to move stolen jewels. And if he was on the right track he'd bet that all of the fantasy vacations came with jewelry as props.

"I have a feeling that you don't have to leave LA to find yourself a harem," Jackie answered with an edge of sarcasm.

"Somehow I don't think that was a compliment."

Mitch grinned. "But to get back on track, how many people do you book to a fantasy?"

"Anywhere from ten to twenty people and then there's myself and my staff," Jackie responded, her tone polished once again. She was not going to give him the satisfaction of her annoyance.

"Then you go on every one of the fantasies. I suppose you run it as a sort of a social director." Mitch knew he could be way off course. But for argument's sake, if Have a Fantasy was also a front for transporting and selling stolen jewels, then it stood to reason that whoever was in charge of the fencing operation would make each trip.

"Something like that," Jackie replied, locking her fingers and pressing her palms against her desk. "I think I should mention that all of our fantasy vacations are rather costly. I can suggest any one of a number of other vacation alternatives."

"Money is no object," Mitch said easily.

"I hope you won't mind my asking, but what do you do for a living?"

"I'm a rhythm and blues musician. I play saxophone." He didn't count that as a full-fledged lie. He did play saxophone.

She patronized with the lift of an eyebrow. "Are you playing somewhere in town?"

"Whenever I feel like it," Mitch condescended to her. "But don't worry, you haven't been wasting your time. I own December's. It's close by to the Brown Derby. Perhaps you've heard of the place?" He didn't own December's but he knew who did.

"I think I may have been there once or twice." Jackie's eyebrow came back down. She knew the club

27

and she'd been there many times. Rhythm and blues was her favorite music, but she didn't want him to know that.

Mitch controlled a smile. He could see that she didn't like the idea that she hadn't gotten away with putting him down. "As I said before, I want to get away and I'd prefer something out of the ordinary." Mitch had the feeling that Jacqueline Lacey was going to prove to be as out of the ordinary as they came. He wondered if she always made herself this unapproachable or was she just trying to be that way with him?

"Our next vacation fantasy is coming up in ten days. It's King Arthur and the Knights of the Round Table." Jackie took a brochure out of her side drawer as she spoke. After spreading it open she turned it to face Mitch.

"I gather it isn't just knights but ladies as well," Mitch said, raising his eyes unexpectedly to catch hers. She let him hold her gaze for a minute before she turned away. He got the impression that she'd been trying to prove some point.

"That's right," Jackie replied coolly. "As you can see, the package includes air fare to London, a connecting flight to Penzance and then a helicopter ride to the Isles of Scilly, which is right off the coast. There are quite a few islands in the group, only five of which are inhabited. We will be staying at one that no longer is. In the 1400s the Earl of Windom built a castle there that the family used as a summer retreat. It remained in the family for generations. When they could no longer manage the upkeep it was turned over to the throne. An American investor bought it up at one time and added sufficient modern improvements with the idea of turning it into a hotel. His loss has become our gain. We rent it out from the government now."

He'd been only half-listening to her recital though he'd concentrated on her fully. Cool and beautiful, he thought. But for all her coolness and all her self-assurance, he had this strange sense of her being just a little bit lost. He had no idea why he would feel that way.

"What about the cost?" he asked, realizing they'd both been silent for a few minutes.

Jackie pointed with the tip of a coral polished nail to the appropriate column. The way he'd just been looking at her set her on edge. She'd had the craziest feeling that those blue eyes of his had been able to see more about her than she wanted him to see.

Mitch noted that the retainer he was working off was not going to cover the tab. Well, it wasn't the first time that he'd had to dig into his own pocket when he was on a case. "Tell me a little more. I'd like to know what I'm getting into besides a suit of armor," he asked, finding her eyes, finding himself wanting to study her more. But she turned her head aside. He knew it was intentional.

"We do get into role playing." Jackie paused and then she looked at him. "Somehow I find it hard to picture you wanting to play chivalrous."

"I'm game as long as you include lessons," Mitch returned, making another try at holding those green eyes of hers but she wouldn't let him.

"There are some things that can't be taught," Jackie answered in a breezy tone. "However, we do offer some lessons. I don't think you'll have any problem with the horses and 'jackasses.' " She'd been wanting

29

to say something cutting to him—something to put him in his place.

Mitch grinned. "I'm going to let you get away with that one because I want to get in a little practice at being chivalrous. But you have sold me on the fantasy. You can write me a ticket. Oh, and I have some friends who might be interested in your other vacation fantasies. If you give me the brochures I'll pass them around."

"Do you always make up your mind this quickly, Mr. Corey?" Jackie asked. No one had ever walked in off the street and booked a fantasy just like that.

"Always, Ms. Lacey." It was Mitch Corey's style to think fast and act fast.

Jackie pulled open the side drawer of her desk and gathered together a string of brochures. She handed them to him. "You can pick your ticket up here anytime after tomorrow and please leave a list of your measurements with our receptionist on your way out," she said coolly.

"And just when I'd given up all hope," Mitch teased, getting to his feet.

"We need the measurements for your costumes." She was not going to give him the satisfaction of seeing any of her annoyance.

Mitch leaned over her desk. "You look like you wish you hadn't done such a good job selling me on the idea."

Agitated, Jackie watched him turn and walk out the door. And then she remembered something that Alex had said a week ago. Maybe she should start to check out the people she booked on each fantasy. Maybe she should start by checking out Mitch Corey. And maybe with some luck she could find a good enough reason to turn him away . . .

CHAPTER TWO

Mitch propped his legs up on the end of a steamer trunk that was designed to act as a coffee table and eased himself back into the cushions of his navy blue corduroy sofa. One nightcap, he promised himself and then he was off to bed. He'd been scrambling all day after leaving Jacqueline Lacey's office, only to come up empty. Well, Mitch thought, tomorrow was another day. And tomorrow, he was going to take along some buying power from the LAPD when he went back to the airlines. It paid to have some friends left at the precinct. A badge bought a lot more information than a private investigator's license and Mitch intended to have a look at the airline rosters for the last few fantasy vacations. He had the dates from the brochures and he was hoping to get a line on Jacqueline Lacey's staff without raising her suspicions. Of course, he knew that he was operating on a far-fetched theory.

Mitch took another long swallow of his nightcap and then the phone rang. He switched the container of milk that he was drinking to his left hand to give his Bulova a look. It was just going on eleven P.M. It wasn't that late, but he was still feeling last night, which had been a late one. Mitch took another large gulp and gave whoever was calling a chance to change their mind. When the ring continued to be persistent, Mitch grudgingly got off the couch and picked up the phone.

"How soon can I bring you over my bills?" Hank Dailey asked on the other end. There was a chortle in his voice. "There's a lady here—and that's in quotes—who wants to say hello to Mitch Corey, the owner of the place." Hank's chortle turned into a laugh.

Mitch groaned. "I hope you covered for me," he said, breaking across Hank's merriment. Hank Dailey was the owner of December's. The lady in quotes couldn't be anyone other than Jacqueline Lacey. Mitch wondered what had brought her around.

"I covered for you, shamus. I told her you were out for the evening."

"Thanks. I owe you one."

"No. I owed you. Now we're even."

"Whatever you say," Mitch smiled and lifted the container of milk to his mouth. He brought it down without taking a drink. "Did she come in alone?"

"She did and if you're not interested and the lady is, I can see to it that she doesn't go home that way."

"You mean she's still there?" Mitch put the container of milk down on a bookcase. Chances were it would remain there, forgotten, until his cleaning lady came in next week or until he traced the smell.

"She sure is," Hank answered. "And it looks like you've got yourself a little more competition than me. From where I'm standing I can see some guy hitting on her at the bar."

"Do me another favor, pal. Show her to my private

33

table. Give her a bottle of your best champagne and tell her I just gave you a ring and I'm on my way in."

"You'd better boogie. She's being flanked on the other side," Hank said, intentionally ribbing. Hank could see that the lady was not having any trouble taking care of herself.

Mitch started to put the phone down and then he pulled it back to his ear, catching Hank before he hung up. "Is it all right with you if I sit in for a set or two?"

"Sure. I'll hand out ear plugs."

"Terrific!" Mitch grinned. "Build my confidence, why don't you?"

Across the line, Hank Dailey laughed.

The smoke-filled club, dimmed by amber light, was crowded, but Mitch knew which direction to look. He saw her before she saw him. She was still dressed the same way as she had been when he'd seen her that morning, except that now she was wearing the jacket to her yellow linen suit. A disc jockey was filling in some recorded dance music, by request, while Hank and the band took a break.

Mitch came up behind Jackie's chair and tapped her on her shoulder. She put down her fluted glass of bubbly. "That's our song," he said, coming around to capture her hands. He drew her to her feet.

"We don't have a song," Jackie responded, surprised at herself for not protesting as Mitch piloted her to the dance floor.

"That's why we had a problem this morning. We didn't have a song. We're going to do much better now." With some gentle pressure at the small of her back, he prompted her to turn into his arms.

Jackie tilted her head to look into Mitch Corey's blue eyes. "What's the name of this song? I don't think I've heard it before."

Mitch smiled. "I have no idea. But it feels right, doesn't it?" She felt better than right and he wasn't even holding her that close. Somewhere in the back of his mind there was a voice suggesting that he think along another line. He ignored it. For the moment, he thought about the heady flush to her cheeks and wondered if it was a trick of the lighting or the champagne.

"You look very sharp this evening," Jackie commented.

He had put on his tuxedo to match Hank and the boys in the band. "I'm a man who's quite willing to wear a tuxedo any day to please a lady." He spoke close to her ear.

"I'll keep that in mind," Jackie answered.

"It's your body I'm after, Ms. Lacey, not your mind," Mitch teased.

"Do women with minds scare you, Mr. Corey?" Jackie followed his movements easily. He was a very good dancer.

Mitch gave her a quick smile. "I don't know yet. Talk to me."

"I don't want to mislead you. I'm not looking for a lover." Jackie decided to make it clear.

"I think I've already arrived at that conclusion," Mitch whispered. "But talk to me anyway."

"What would you like me to talk about?" It had been a stupid idea to come. She'd known that as soon as she'd arrived. She didn't know why she had stayed to wait for him.

Mitch brought Jackie closer. Jackie felt herself tense but she didn't pull away. "Talk to me about you," Mitch suggested. "You can tell me first whether you like to be called Jacqueline or Jackie." He hadn't picked up much information on her. All he knew so far was that she had an apartment out in Santa Monica and that she lived alone. And that she was twenty-eight years old, just about what he'd guessed. He'd gotten verification from her driver's license after a phone call to a friend.

"I think it would be better if we kept it Ms. Lacey and Mr. Corey." She tried not to inhale too deeply the heady scent of his masculine cologne.

The song they had been dancing to ended. The disc jockey called out for another request. Mitch held Jackie close to him until she took the initiative and disengaged herself.

"Why would it be a better idea to keep it Ms. Lacey and Mr. Corey?" Mitch asked smoothly as they walked back to the table.

Jackie didn't bother to answer. When they got to the table she picked up her yellow leather clutch bag. "I really do have to be going. Thank you for the champagne and the dance," she said formally. She didn't see any reason to prolong his pitch. Not when she'd already made herself clear. Obviously, he had a problem with listening. Or maybe he just wasn't used to getting no for an answer.

"You can't leave yet. You haven't heard me play." He took her clutch bag out from under her arm and set it back down on the table.

"I thought that was what you were doing." Jackie gave him a sophisticated look.

"That was just a little foreplay. Coming up is the real thing." Mitch grinned.

"Are you going to play your saxophone now?" Jackie challenged.

"First I have to wet my throat, Ms. Lacey, and then I'll play you some sweet music. You did come to hear me play, didn't you? Or was there some other reason that you couldn't wait the ten days until we met again?" He knew he was giving her a hard time, but she'd had her turn in the afternoon.

Jackie sat down. "I prefer Jackie to Jacqueline." She was not going to run off leaving him thinking what he was thinking.

Mitch lifted the champagne out of an ice-filled bucket and poured for both of them. He had expected her to make some loud disclaimer and leave. "I like Mitch better than Mr. Corey," he said. He found it was difficult to get a line on her. As soon as he thought he had her in a box, she pushed at the corners.

"How long have you had this place?" Jackie asked, looking around. Hank Dailey and his band were tuning up.

Mitch followed the direction of Jackie's gaze and swapped a smile with Hank who was glancing his way. "I've had the club for a while," he answered. She turned back to him. "Which one was it?" he asked.

"Which one was what?"

"Did you come to hear me play? Or did you have another reason?" He took a swallow of his champagne.

"I came here to check you out," Jackie answered

matter-of-factly. She picked up her glass and drank some of her champagne.

"I can get you a written recommendation if you like. But I thought you just told me that I wasn't in the running." He knew perfectly well that wasn't what she meant. But what had sent her here to check up on him?

"I'm not checking you out because I'm interested in sleeping with you. My partner thinks we should start to check out the people we book on our fantasy vacations, since for the most part the settings we use are fairly secluded."

"I wouldn't let you sleep," Mitch said, relaxing.

Jackie didn't pick up his implication at first. Then she did. "Do you always come on this strong?"

For all his reputation, earned and unearned, Mitch didn't usually come on strong at all. He just responded to the signals that existed when the chemistry was right. Jacqueline Lacey had a chemistry all her own. With somewhat of a shock, Mitch realized that he was starting to have to put up a fight to ignore it. "Would you believe me if I said no?" He didn't expect that she would, but it was about the only whole truth he'd given her so far.

"Would you give me a few days to think about it?" Jackie smiled blandly. Every now and then she noticed something in his blue eyes—a sort of world-weariness, as if he'd been through everything, not once, but twice and he hadn't been happy either time. It was a look that was at odds with his flip, easygoing manner. That look was in his eyes now.

Whatever Jacqueline was really thinking, she'd perfected the art of keeping it to herself. Mitch had the funny feeling that in some ways they were very much alike.

"You're an unusual lady, Jacqueline Lacey," he said.

"I live an unusual life. I don't suppose there are too many people who spend most of their time in a fantasy."

Mitch rolled his blue eyes outrageously. "Personally speaking, I spend quite a bit of my own time fantasizing."

"In your case, I'd see a doctor. Perhaps you'll find out that most women don't care to be treated as sex objects."

"I'll take it that I've been properly chastised." Mitch put on a dolefully contrived look. "Maybe we should get on some safe ground. Why don't you tell me about your partner?" It was about time he got around to interrogating her.

Jackie took another sip of champagne and gave him a keen look. "Why would my partner interest you?"

"You're doing your checking. I'm doing mine," Mitch answered easily. "Should I number your partner as competition?" He already knew that Alex Shaffner was in his late forties and that he was married. For a second, Mitch felt crummy being underhanded with her. But then a conscience was low on his list of priorities.

"Alex is married . . . happily, I might add. And might I add again that I didn't come here this evening because I was looking to start up a relationship."

"Don't tell me you're only interested in one-night stands," Mitch said, pushing the game around one more time.

"Don't tell me that you're interested in more," Jackie returned dryly.

"What about you? Do you have a special man in your life?" She had his number all right. He did take his intimacies in small doses.

"No," Jackie answered coolly, checking her watch. It was a little past midnight—high time she left.

Mitch knew that she meant to cut loose. "On that note, I think I will go and play for you. Only you do have to make me a promise." He got to his feet.

"What promise?"

"That you'll still be here when I finish."

Jackie gave Mitch a cosmopolitan smile. "I never walk out in the middle of a performance."

Mitch showed her with his blue eyes that he hadn't had any problem deciphering her implication. "This is only Act One. I really get going in Act Two and I do promise a happy ending. But I can't blame you if you don't trust me completely." He had a crazy urge to tell her not to trust him at all.

"Don't let it go to your head, but I wouldn't trust you as far as I could throw you," Jackie answered glibly.

"Maybe I should check out your muscles," Mitch countered.

Jackie laughed. Then she gave him a what-am-I-going-to-do-with-you look. "Maybe you should just go and play your saxophone."

"I'm going to be keeping my eyes on you," Mitch warned. "If you walk out, you're going to be chased by a lunatic with a saxophone dangling from his neck." He started to leave the table, then he stopped and looked back.

"I'm going to stay and listen to your music," Jackie said, waving him off. She decided she would stay for a few minutes and then she would leave.

After a huddle with Hank Dailey, Mitch sat in and played a sampling of his old-time favorite rhythm and blues numbers. The selections included "Blue Moon," "Oh, Lady, Be Good," and "Don't Blame Me (for Falling in Love with You)." True to his word, Mitch kept his eyes on Jackie all the way through.

Jackie wasn't as true to herself. She was still sitting at the table when Mitch returned, telling herself that she just couldn't walk out. It wouldn't have been very polite. More accurately, she hadn't been able to persuade herself to leave off seeing Mitch Corey's entire sexy performance. The man did have a way with his saxophone. Of course, Jackie had absolutely no doubt that the effect he had on her was only temporary.

"You are good," she praised, glancing away from him and noting as she did that he had the full attention of each and every woman in the room.

Mitch smiled. "I was hoping that you'd find that I had at least one redeeming quality."

She didn't consider any of his qualities at all redeeming. In fact the quality he'd just displayed left her feeling uncomfortably edgy. She assured herself that didn't mean she was attracted to him. She was positive that she wasn't attracted to him. She was unequivocally certain about that, as certain as she was that it was time to go home. "On that note, I think it is definitely time I left."

Mitch got to his feet as she did. There wasn't any question that she meant it this time. "I'll see you home."

41

"I have my car and I can see myself home," Jackie said firmly.

"How about seeing me home then? My car is being repaired," he kidded, walking with her through the club.

"Don't you ever call it quits?" The sharp agitation that she'd been feeling on and off since she'd met him showed in her eyes.

For a crazy second, Mitch Corey considered calling it quits. But he knew he wouldn't.

"No," Mitch answered, coming up with a smile that didn't quite make it. *Watch out for me, Jacqueline Lacey . . . I'm coming after you,* he said, but he didn't say it out loud.

CHAPTER THREE

The forest air held the warm morning scent of trees and wildflowers. Jackie sat sidesaddle on a black stallion that was blanketed with the emblem and colors of King Arthur's court. A woven purple wool cape billowed out behind her. She shrugged free of the hood of her riding cape and her long, luxurious honey-blond hair caught the wind.

Horse and rider descended a steep incline. She couldn't yet see the small lake that was up ahead. It was so hidden, she thought for sure that she was the only one to have discovered it. She called it the Pool of Pendragon and she always came a day ahead of her staff to enjoy its special cool. This was her favorite fantasy tour—this was her favorite fantasy.

Mitch had just finished climbing a large dune in his search for the castle when he saw her riding up. He took cover behind a heavy thicket of bushes and trees.

Jackie reined in her stallion and dismounted. She looked his way once as she took off her cape, but she didn't see him. He didn't intend that she should. For her notice, he planned on establishing his presence tomorrow afternoon with the other vacationers.

Jackie slipped off her leather sandals and wiggled

her toes in the grassy carpet beneath her feet. She unfastened her outer garment gown of embroidered cloth far enough down so that she could take it off easily. She lifted her face to the sun as she lowered the straps of a loose-fitting cotton tunic. The tunic fell to her ankles and she stepped out of it.

The sun, filtering through the tree branches, drew patterns on her statuesque form, highlighting her in a very contemporary pink bikini. She retied her top. It had come loose during her ride. As she did, Jackie remembered that the ties on this particular bathing suit top always came annoyingly loose when she swam. She fingered each tie for a moment and then with a small smile playing on her lips, Jackie took her top off, letting an impulse have its way.

Mitch Corey felt his breath actually get stuck in his throat. His blue eyes slipped over her. She was unbelievably beautiful. And he realized, very pointedly, that he was being an unbelievable heel.

Jackie walked to the lake, dipping one foot in first before diving beneath the surface. She rose with the satin swath of her blond hair trailing the water and began a leisurely stroke.

It was rare, but every now and then, Mitch did reflect on the possibility that he had some sense of decency, even perhaps an interest in fair play. He was having one of those rare moments now. He even went as far as ordering himself to leave her to her privacy, but the only motion he managed was to grind out the cigarette he had just lit.

After a while, Jackie floated on her back and daydreamed. On a magical day like this it was easy to drift into a fantasy. In her mind, there came a knight in shining armor—a knight who was the greatest of them all and she was Queen Guinevere. "My Lady," spoke Sir Lancelot. "I shall forever defend your honor and keep you safe. I pledge myself to be your champion and I offer you my love and devotion to my dying day." Jackie opened her eyes and laughed ruefully. Fantasies never turned into realities but she was at least smart enough to turn them into a profit.

Mitch wasn't that far away that he couldn't hear her laugh. Independent of any mental directive, he stepped clear of the bush and walked up to where she'd dropped her clothing.

Jackie stopped abruptly in the middle of a swimming stroke. She thought she'd heard something or sensed something. Turning toward the shore, Jackie looked around. And then she saw him.

Mitch angled a glance at her.

Her green eyes astonished, Jackie stared back. She opened her mouth to speak but nothing came out.

He saw her start to shiver. "I think you should come out of the water. You look cold."

"What are you doing here?" She finally got back the power of speech.

"Come out of the water and I'll tell you." He had no idea what he was going to come up with to tell her.

"I-I'm not . . ." Jackie started to say that she didn't have the top of her bathing suit on and then she realized he probably already knew that. Shock gave way to fury.

Mitch could see her getting mad. "Don't worry, I'll turn my back."

"That's really decent of you," Jackie said sarcastically.

"Come on, Jackie. I am sorry. You're going to get sick if you stay in the water shivering like that."

Jackie watched him turn his back to her and then raise his hand to cover his eyes. Oh, she'd just bet he was sorry! What was he doing here anyway?

Steeling herself, Jackie swam to the edge of the lake. She drew in a few deep breaths trying to settle herself and then she came out of the water with her arm in front of her breasts.

He heard her coming up to him. He was still standing right next to her clothes. She didn't say a word but he could feel her anger.

Jackie picked up the top of her bathing suit. Watching him warily, she tied the strings around her back and then over her shoulders.

"Decent?" Mitch asked. He didn't wait for her to answer. Out of the corner of his eye he could see that she was and so he swung around to her.

Jackie made eye contact with him. Then with the strength of her whole body behind her hand she slapped his face. He kind of yelped as she caught him off guard. "Now what are you doing here? The fantasy doesn't begin until tomorrow."

"Do you feel better now?" Mitch asked, testing the mobility of his jaw.

"What are you doing here?" Jackie repeated tersely.

Mitch evaded her. "Where's your towel?" He looked around for one while he tried to think up an answer. The answer was giving him as much of a problem as trying to figure out why he'd let her know that he was here in the first place. Dumb move, Corey . . .

"I didn't bring one," Jackie said tightly. "I want to know why you are here. How did you even get here?"

Mitch picked up her tunic and handed it to her. "Put this on." He let her find his eyes. He could see in hers that she was not going to be put off any longer.

Jackie stepped into her tunic. "I don't understand this. I sold you a ticket for a flight to London for tomorrow."

"I traded it in. Actually I came two days early. I've been staying in St. Mary's," he lied. The truth was that he'd been on the same night flight with her to London and he'd made the same connecting flight early this morning with her to Penzance. Naturally, he had been in disguise. She'd taken a helicopter from there to her fantasy island. He'd taken another helicopter to St. Mary's and rented a motor boat to get him here. "I rented a motor boat and came over to sneak a look at the castle. I saw you in the water as I was tramping around."

She looked at him suspiciously. "If you were in St. Mary's yesterday, why did you wait for today to take a sneak look at the castle?"

"I went fishing yesterday."

"Fishing? Somehow, I don't picture you going fishing—not for fish." Jackie studied him closely while she twirled her hair, wringing out some of the water.

"How do you picture me?" Without warning, Mitch raised his arms and yanked off his blue knit pullover.

"What do you think you are doing?" Her eyes widened and then narrowed.

Mitch smiled. "Don't panic. I'm just trying to help you out. Here, my lady, dry your hair." He handed her his shirt.

"The sun will dry it," Jackie answered, feeling a little embarrassed at having jumped to the wrong con-

47

clusion. Then feeling more embarrassed as he caught her eyes gliding over the strong masculine expanse of his bare chest.

"True, but a knight who begs forgiveness asks to do the lady a service." He moved behind her. Without her invitation, he held her hair in his hand and felt the wet silken weight before enfolding it in his shirt to wipe at it gently. She didn't stop him. He took his time.

"Your shirt will be all wet, Sir Knight," Jackie said, not sure why she was letting him minister to her or why she wasn't feeling as angry anymore as she knew she should be.

"It's all right. I don't mind." The material of her tunic clung to the dampness of her body. "Turn to me, my lady," Mitch whispered.

Jackie slowly pivoted around to him. "I haven't forgiven you," she said.

Mitch let his shirt fall to the grass. "I know," he whispered, placing his hands loosely on her hips.

She raised her gaze up at him. He gave her a lazy smile. He wanted to kiss her. He knew that she knew it and was deciding if she was going to object or not. And then he saw something else: Before she lowered her lashes, giving him permission, he thought he saw a kind of shyness in her eyes.

He found her mouth. She made no attempt to hold him. He wanted to draw her closer but he didn't. He kept his hands on her hips. Butterfly soft, her lips moved under his.

His kiss was a whole series of kisses, each one feathery. He nibbled on her bottom lip. His mouth inched around hers, taking the corners one at a time. There was no pressure or demand. She felt as if he were becoming acquainted with her mouth and giving her the chance to get acquainted with his. Jackie wanted to hold on to him. She was starting to feel as if she needed to hold on to him. His kisses were making her feel light-headed. She wished he were wearing his shirt.

He wasn't quite sure why he was kissing her this way. He'd meant to give her one thorough kiss and get it out of his system. But the minute his mouth touched hers, he hadn't felt like hurrying.

Her bottom lip trembled before she accepted the gentle exploration of his tongue. Mitch felt her hands come up slowly to loop around his neck. He brought her closer, even as he was telling himself to pull back.

Through the dampness of her tunic, Jackie could feel the heat of his bare chest. Her mind was spinning wildly and her pulse raced. She slid her fingers into his hair. Her breasts were grazing against him. Her whole body was swaying without volition.

Mitch ran his hands down over her hips. Then trailing unchecked, he ran his hands up her sides. He tried coaxing her tongue into his mouth while his own tongue was crazily tasting the sweetness of her. She started to follow his lead, then suddenly objected.

Jackie uncurled her hands from around his neck and pressed her palms to his shoulders. Her movements were rapid, panicked. She was trembling as he released her. Quickly, she turned her back to him. When had any man made her tremble this way before?

Mitch stood there facing the back of her. He'd kissed her. No big deal. My God! He was all shaken up over a kiss.

49

They stayed that way, the two of them fighting to reject the feelings that they had just shared, each reasoning away the sensation.

After long minutes, Mitch raised his hands to turn her around to him but she was already doing that on her own.

"I'm not going to get involved with you," Jackie said fiercely, firmly, wanting it understood that he had gotten as much as she was going to give and that she was not going to give any more.

Mitch let a second go by before he spoke. "I bet you have to say that at least a dozen times a week," he quipped, knowing that kidding around with her was the best way to put distance between them—if distance was what he wanted.

"I bet you hear it at least that often," Jackie countered. Her equilibrium almost restored, she gave him a quick upward glance with cool eyes.

"Only when I'm listening," Mitch teased, watching her reach down for her gown. "I was thinking," he said as she stepped into it, shoving her tunic inside. "Since I'm here, what do you say to showing me the castle?"

Jackie pushed her hands through the sleeves. She looked at him with her head tipped to one side. "I suppose if I don't, you'll hunt around until you find it on your own."

Mitch tried out a smile on her as he nodded his head.

"All right," Jackie agreed without returning his smile. She'd thought of flat out refusing, but she was not going to give him the idea that she might be con-

cerned about being with him. She wasn't concerned . . .

She had trouble closing the brass buckle fastenings
on her gown because her hands were shaking. Even so,
she kept assuring herself that she would easily forget
his kiss. She didn't need any man in her life. She was
exactly the way she wanted to be: independent and on
her way to making a lot of money. Jacqueline Lacey
did not intend on ever giving away any pieces of her
heart.

Mitch picked up his polo shirt and pulled it on over
his head. It was damp and it clung to his skin, as did
the scent of her hair. He didn't let himself breathe too
deeply.

Jackie tied her cape on and then walked to her
horse. Mitch followed after her.

"Do you know how to ride?" Jackie patted the stallion's neck, disrupting the horse from busily chewing
up clumps of tall grass.

Mitch nodded his head. "I'll get on first and then
I'll pull you up."

Jackie watched Mitch hoist himself up into the saddle. He kicked a foot free from one of the stirrups and
stretched his hand out to her.

Using the stirrup as a step, Jackie gripped his forearm while he firmly held hers. She felt strong hard
muscle flex beneath her fingers as he pulled her astride
the saddle in front of him.

Jackie faced front sitting as far away from him as
she could.

Mitch took hold of the reins, his arms encircling
her. "Come closer to me and put your hand around
my back," he instructed.

"I'm fine," Jackie answered with a toss of her head.

The stallion shifted restlessly beneath them as Mitch held the reins in check. "I don't feel you sitting secure."

"I am secure," Jackie insisted, becoming annoyed and agitated.

Mitch switched the reins to one hand and leaned forward. "I'm not trying to compromise you."

He said it solemnly but she sensed his amusement. "I think you would try anything," she accused icily.

"Probably, but not on top of a horse," Mitch teased, keeping the stallion steady.

"I don't find your humor amusing." Jackie shot him a deprecating look.

Mitch grinned. "Put your arm around my back so that I don't have to worry about you falling off. I'm sure you don't want me to start thinking that you're afraid to be too close to me."

"I guess chivalry isn't dead," Jackie responded sarcastically as she placed her arm around him.

Mitch kicked his heels into the stallion's flanks, sending the silky strands of her blond hair blowing across his neck. Her shoulders rubbed up against his chest as she stayed in place. He tried to concentrate on the scenery.

Jackie could feel the dampness of his shirt touching her side. She could feel the rippling of his muscles under her hand and the nudge of his masculine knee hitting up against her leg. She sat so tight and erect that her back ached.

Mitch guided the horse across a small bridge that spanned an even smaller moat. With a twist of the reins, Mitch drew the horse to a halt in a courtyard in front of a stone castle.

Jackie slid down from the stallion before he had the chance to offer her his assistance.

Mitch agilely swung out of the saddle.

"You ride well," Jackie said, releasing a deep breath to force the tension out of her body.

"I once considered becoming a rodeo rider."

"What made you change your mind?" Jackie led the way into the castle.

"Broken bones and bruises."

"Oh . . ." She couldn't think of any other comment.

Mitch blinked his eyes to get accustomed to the dimmer light once they were inside. They stood in a wide entry. The air was still but not dank or unpleasant. The walls, ceiling, and floor were all constructed of irregularly set stone. Unlit tapers lined the walls. Foot-wide slit openings sent in blotches of sunlight.

"I'm going to get changed. Then I'll take you on a tour," Jackie said breezily.

"Okay." Mitch looked after her as she walked to a wide stone staircase to his left. He walked further down the hall to look at some tapestries and to think cool thoughts.

It took Jackie less than ten minutes to change into jeans and a shirt. She brushed her hair and crossed it back into a single braid. There was no way that she was going to let Mitch Corey affect her. Not her! She was too smart for that.

Mitch turned from the tapestry he'd been studying to watch her approach.

"Do you like them?" Jackie asked politely.

53

"Very much," Mitch answered idly. He could see that he was going to get the formal treatment.

"Before I take you around, I thought you might like something to eat." She thought she sounded like a museum guide.

He'd looked at his watch when she'd gone to change. It had been four thirty then. He knew she'd only had a danish and coffee in the morning on the plane and unless she'd grabbed something to eat before she'd gone for her swim, she probably hadn't had any lunch. He'd bought two large bags of fish and chips and he'd eaten his way through both of them while he'd steered the motor boat from St. Mary's. He wasn't hungry. "Now that you mention food, I'm starving."

Jackie directed the way. "My staff won't be here until the morning. All the foods have been delivered, but I'm not much of a cook. I hope you won't mind peanut butter and jelly on whole wheat bread."

"Sounds good, as long as you've got milk to go along with it." He could feel the roof of his mouth start to stick.

"How about a chilled bottle of white wine instead?" Jackie led him down a hall toward the kitchen.

"Decadence before the sun sets? I'm surprised at you," Mitch said, teasing. He couldn't handle any more of her stilted conversation.

"Champagne is decadence, not white wine," Jackie rejoined.

"I'll keep that in mind." He gave her a wink.

They entered an oversized kitchen. He took note that there was a commercial-size stove, a huge sink, and a fireplace over which an accumulation of pots

54

were hung. In addition, there was a long wooden table and wooden chairs. "I don't see a refrigerator," Mitch remarked.

"There's an ice room out back," Jackie answered before going into a pantry for the peanut butter, jam, and bread.

"Aha." Mitch nodded his head. "I know how the sink works because you have plumbing, but what about the stove?"

"Propane gas tanks," Jackie replied, setting the fixings for their sandwiches on the table along with pewter plates and goblets. "Now why don't you sit down and I'll go get the wine."

"Tell me where to look and I'll go," Mitch offered.

"That's okay. It will be easier for me to find it."

Mitch pulled out a chair, turned it around and straddled it. "I get the feeling that you don't like having a man do for you," he tossed out as she started to leave.

"I'm sure you know how to find plenty of women who do," Jackie tossed back on her way out.

He knew more about her now. For example, he knew that in the past few days she'd been keeping herself busy with some hotshot movie director, Victor Logan. She'd had lunch with him Tuesday and Wednesday and then dinner with him Friday night. At least he'd brought her home at a decent hour and he hadn't stayed. Not for nothing, but the guy was old enough to be her father. He wasn't her father, though. Mitch knew because he'd checked. What the hell made her want to run around with an old man?

Jackie returned with the wine and a corkscrew.

"Here, you can open the wine for me. I don't want you to get out of practice."

Mitch grinned and obliged. He expertly uncorked the wine and filled both of their goblets. "How'd you get into the vacation fantasy business?" he asked.

"I met Alex Shaffner a few years ago at a party. He had the agency and he was looking for a partner. The agency was making out all right, but Alex had some debts and he needed some money. I had a small inheritance and I bought in. I was looking for something to do that would allow me to be creative and to feel challenged. I'd been in and out of a few things but I hadn't found anything that felt right and, more important, was sufficiently lucrative."

A flag came up: "What do you term sufficiently lucrative?"

She turned her green eyes on him. "I suppose sufficient isn't quite the right word. I'm out to make as much money as I can. Being in business yourself, I'm sure you have the same drive."

Mitch manufactured a smile of agreement. Sure, he had an identical drive. But was her ride taking her along a straight and narrow path? "Is this tour business lucrative enough?"

"It's starting to be."

Did that mean that she'd added more tours or had she added fencing jewels as a sideline? "What other things were you into before this?"

She spread peanut butter on two slices of bread. "Just things." There were things that she would tell him and things that she would not tell him. "Do you like a lot of jelly?"

Mitch nodded his head. If he let them, those eyes of

56

hers could send him walking up a wall. "How about this . . . You tell me about you and I'll tell you about me?" He lifted his goblet to his lips and tasted the wine. He hadn't recognized the label but it was a grade-A grape.

"How about you tell me about you first?" Jackie volleyed as she handed him a sandwich.

"You can ask me anything. I'm my favorite subject." Mitch took a bite of his sandwich and then a healthy swallow of wine. He watched her do the same.

"Okay," Jackie said, eyeing him. "I'll start with an easy one. Are you a native Californian?"

"A native Californian? Of course not." Mitch smiled. "Is anyone? I was born in Dallas."

"I was born in LA," Jackie said.

"Really!" He already knew that. "Ever think of going into the movies?" He wanted to think that was why she'd let herself be entertained by Vic Logan.

"No," Jackie answered. "I bet you must have come to LA to get into pictures yourself."

"Would I fare better with you if I were an actor?" He thought of Vic Logan again and suddenly felt jealous.

"Worse." Jackie took a sip of her wine.

"Why worse?" He watched her with total concentration.

"I was once married to an actor."

She took him by surprise. He hadn't known that she'd been married. "Anyone I would know?"

"I doubt it. He hasn't made it big yet, but from what I hear, he's still trying."

"What's his name?" He offered to fill her goblet

57

again but she covered the rim with her palm. He filled his.

"Gregg Allen."

"Doesn't ring any bell."

"What about you?" Jackie asked. "Have you ever been married?" She finished eating the last of her sandwich.

Mitch thought of saying no and leaving it at that. He didn't care to discuss his marriage. "An actress," he answered. "She was just starting out at the time and very eager for success." Mitch decided not to lie to her unless he had to.

"Did she make it big?" Jackie asked. She noticed that world-weariness in his blue eyes.

"All the way to the top," Mitch answered, taking a full swallow of wine.

Jackie thought of asking for her name, then changed her mind. She could see that he didn't want to talk about his marriage. She didn't want to talk about hers either. "I like your music," she said, meaning it but saying it to break the abrupt silence.

"Do you?"

She heard the smile in his voice. "Yes," she answered. "I especially liked the way you played 'Blue Moon.'"

"Do you have a dream in your heart, Jacqueline Lacey?" He used the song.

"Dreams are for dreamers," Jackie answered, nonchalant.

"Are you a dreamer?" His eyes stayed on her.

"No," Jackie lied. She didn't like him probing to know more about her than she chose for him to know.

Mitch could feel her getting suddenly uptight.

"Why don't you give me the grand tour now," he suggested, his voice casual.

The tour she gave him took over an hour. The castle had at least a dozen wings—more, maybe. And at least one secret tunnel.

"I didn't see any suits of armor around," he commented. They were in a chamber that she'd said would be his during his stay. She had not indicated which chamber was hers.

"My staff will be bringing them along with everything else we'll need. I've brought only what the ladies will wear," Jackie answered, following every flicker of his blue eyes as he looked around.

His eyes came back to her. "It must be annoying for you to travel with all of that."

"The ladies' costumes, you mean?"

"Yes," Mitch answered.

"It's really not any big problem. The studio sends what I've picked out to the office and Alex always helps me to the airport."

"It must give the customs inspectors a turn when you go through with all that fake jewelry," Mitch commented, his eyes on her face.

"Not really," Jackie answered. "They hardly look. They're used to me by now."

It was just about the way he figured it, if he figured it right. "What time will your staff be arriving tomorrow?"

"Around ten o'clock in the morning," Jackie responded. "And now I think it's time you started back for St. Mary's. In a while the water begins to get very choppy."

Mitch walked with her out of the chamber and into

a hall. The hall was surrounded by a parapet which gave the open-air effect of a balcony.

"I don't feel right knowing that you're here spending the night all alone," Mitch said. "I'm worried about you. Maybe I should stay to make sure you're safe."

"I'll be perfectly safe. There's an older gentleman who is a caretaker on the premises. He lives here year round and takes charge of the horses." She knew he was trying to finesse his way into staying and she had no intention of letting him.

They started down a set of stairs side by side, but not touching. Mitch slanted his head to her. "A caretaker, she says . . . Don't you ever watch scary movies? Caretakers are never safe."

"I'll take my chances." Jackie gave him the smile he had earned.

He could see that she wasn't going to be pushed or he would have continued to try.

They reached the bottom of the stairs. "I'll be back early in the morning to check on you," he told her.

"How early?" Jackie walked him to the door.

"Don't worry about setting your alarm clock. I'll wake you if you're not up."

"Don't bother looking forward to waking me," Jackie countered. "I'll be up early."

Mitch opened the castle door. Jackie stepped outside with him.

"Take the path over there." She pointed. "It will take you straight to the water."

Mitch took hold of her hand and raised it to his lips. "Good night, my lady. Sleep well," he whispered.

60

"Good night, my lord," Jackie murmured. "I hope you sleep well also."

"I'm going to give it my best," Mitch said, turning away. But he already knew he was going to spend his night thinking about her.

CHAPTER FOUR

The next morning Jackie set four slices of bread in the toaster. Mitch looked past her shoulder at the copper pots hanging over the fireplace. But the distraction didn't work. His eyes kept coming back to her. She wore loose-fitting khaki-colored shorts—the kind that were meant to come off casual rather than sexy—and a yellow T-shirt. She had her hair tied back with a yellow and white striped scarf. He was finding it hard to keep believing anything bad about her even with some of his theory adding up.

"How was the water going back last night?" Jackie asked. She didn't think it showed but she was all tense and on edge this morning.

"Choppy," Mitch answered. He hadn't gone back to St. Mary's. He'd spent the night stretched out in the motor boat watching to see if she had any visitors. She hadn't. In the morning, he'd changed into a clean plaid shirt, tan slacks, and he'd shaved with a straight-edged razor before walking back to the castle.

Jackie cracked the first of four eggs into a bowl. Out of the corner of her eye, she saw him start to walk around.

"Did you sleep well?" Mitch asked.

"Yes," Jackie answered. But she hadn't slept well at all. She'd dreamt about him—long passionate love dreams that still left wild feelings inside of her.

Jackie cracked the last of the four eggs. "I like my eggs scrambled. Is that all right with you?" She slid a glance at him and he nodded his head. He was standing right next to her.

Fascinated, Mitch watched the way the light from a window streaked the strands of her honey-blond hair. Before he thought about it, he reached out and untied her scarf, tossing it to the counter. Jackie's breath caught. Mitch ran his fingers through her silken strands. She stood motionless. He touched her cheek and then she slowly turned.

"I like your hair loose," Mitch whispered.

Her breath was still caught in her throat as she raised her eyes to find his. There was something in his gaze that she had not seen before—something she hadn't expected. There was a tenderness there that touched her in a way she didn't want to be touched. This couldn't be happening to her! She wouldn't let it happen . . .

"It's not practical," Jackie answered quickly. She grabbed her scarf, hoping he didn't notice her hands trembling as she tied it back on.

"I don't suppose that it would be," Mitch said.

He walked away from her, distancing himself. He knew she hadn't realized it, but the look they'd just shared had disconcerted him as well. He'd seen something in her eyes too. There had been a vulnerability in her gaze so fleeting that he couldn't be absolutely certain he'd seen it, yet he felt it. It was a look that both excited and agitated him. The detective in him wanted to see her as a lady who was cold as ice. If his suspicion about her turned out to be true, he wanted to be able to walk away clean.

Maybe he was feeling vulnerable himself?

Intent on denying that possibility, he casually walked back to her. The toast had burned. Mitch noticed the scowl on her face as she went to take the scorched bread out with the tips of her fingers. She winced.

"Here, let me do that," Mitch said. Quickly moving her hands aside, he took the burned bread out of the toaster and tossed it in the trash. "Are you okay?" he asked, taking her hands.

"Fine," Jackie answered, pulling her hands away from him. She popped four more slices in the toaster.

Mitch leaned back negligently against the counter. "Scrambled eggs and peanut butter and jelly sandwiches . . . Is that the extent of your diet?" he teased.

"On some days." Jackie tried to keep her tone light in response to his.

"What about the other days?" There was an undercurrent of sexual tension between them. He felt it. He knew she felt it too.

"I order in or I eat out." With a shaky hand, Jackie picked up a wire whisk from the counter to beat the eggs. It fell and landed on the stone floor. Her eyes rushed to him.

Mitch bent and picked it up. "Why so tense?" he asked, knowing why.

Their eyes locked. She thought he was going to kiss her. She turned away and began to beat the eggs.

"I have a lot on my mind," Jackie said in a clipped

tone, determined to regain her equilibrium. Avoiding his unrelenting blue eyes, she whipped the eggs with a fury.

Mitch's jaw tightened. That was the issue. What kind of things did she have on her mind? And that was exactly what he asked her.

Jackie gave him an impatient look. The expression on his face confused her, as did the tone of his voice. It should have been a perfect come-on line, only he'd asked it almost accusatorially. She simply couldn't figure him out.

If he was trying a new angle, it wasn't going to work. At least that was what she tried to tell herself. But the disturbing truth was that Mitch Corey was getting under her skin.

Jackie turned her full concentration on getting the eggs scrambled and breakfast over. She wanted to end these intimate moments alone with him. She just knew that once her staff and the others arrived, she'd be able to get back in gear.

Jackie dished the eggs onto two plates. She turned with both of them in her hands. Mitch came up and flipped the bar of the toaster, just in time to save the four new slices of bread from burning. He followed her to the table and took a seat opposite her.

Her eyes flickered over him as he started to eat. "After my staff is settled, I'll have someone follow you back to St. Mary's with one of our boats so that you can return the one you rented."

Mitch shrugged his acceptance as he buttered a slice of toast. He was noticing that she was holding her fork but only toying with her eggs.

Jackie put down her fork and reached for the coffee

pot that she'd set on the table earlier. Mitch put his hand on it first, filling her cup and then his. She deliberately avoided his eyes.

"The eggs are just right," Mitch said, bringing another forkful to his mouth. He watched her sip her coffee, ignoring what was on her plate.

Jackie nodded her head and regarded him silently for a second.

"Your eggs are going to get cold," he said.

Jackie picked her fork back up and managed to eat a little. She had absolutely no appetite. Her stomach was tied in knots.

Mitch finished off the last of his eggs. "Would you like me to butter you a slice of toast?"

"No, thank you."

"Aren't you hungry?"

"I thought I was," Jackie responded. "I should know by now that I always get all tense and jittery before the start of each fantasy tour." She hoped he would believe that lie. He was the reason she was tense and jittery.

Mitch lifted his cup of coffee and took a swallow. He wanted to think that was all there was to it—that and the other kind of tension there was still between them. "I think I know a way to calm you down." He got to his feet. "I'll be right back."

"Where are you . . ." Jackie let the sentence drop and watched him leave. He'd changed the tempo between them and she wasn't at all sure how to handle him now. Up until now, his come-on hadn't felt real.

Jackie stood up, took a deep breath, and gathered the dishes to take to the sink. She hoped he was bringing her two aspirins. Her head was starting to pound. Or was it just her heart that was behaving badly?

Mitch came back with his saxophone hanging from a leather strap around his neck.

Still running the dishes under the faucet, Jackie turned her head.

"This is a guaranteed cure for the jitters," Mitch said.

She looked down at his saxophone and then up to meet his eyes. The cup and saucer she was holding rattled against each other as she watched his mouth curve with a sexy smile. Oh, she knew exactly what he was up to . . . Act Two was moving right along. What did she have to do to make him understand that she did not want to be pursued?

"Shall I take off my shirt," Mitch teased. "Or do you have a towel to wipe your hands?"

"I have a towel." Jackie gave him a cool look. "And after I finish the dishes, I'll use it."

Mitch walked up. Holding his saxophone aside, he turned the water off. "You can do the dishes later. Union rules—I can't play unless I have your full concentration." He took the cup and saucer away from her and laid them in the sink.

"I don't have time for this," Jackie insisted.

"We'll make time," Mitch persisted.

Jackie could see from his expression that he wouldn't take no for an answer. With a resolute sigh, she wiped her hands. "Okay," she said, laying the towel on the counter and crossing her arms.

"That's no way to relax," Mitch chastised. Moving his saxophone to his side, he slipped his free arm around her waist and guided her to the table. Jackie

67

moved reluctantly. Relaxing was the last thing Jacqueline Lacey intended to do around Mitch Corey.

Mitch let go of Jackie's waist to swing a chair around for her. "My lady," he said.

Jackie obediently sat down.

Mitch swung a second chair out. He positioned it sideways in front of her and set his foot on it. His trousers creased tight around the hard muscles of his thigh. With studied casualness, he lodged the saxophone against his leg. And then he slowly wet his lips with his tongue.

Even though she tried furiously not to, Jackie's eyes fixed on Mitch's very masculine mouth. She swallowed convulsively, recalling in vivid detail the sensation of his kiss. Quick shivers went through her body. She managed to keep it from showing in her face.

Mitch tasted the mouthpiece of his horn and then thoughtfully pressed it against his jaw. "You don't look like you're even trying to relax," he admonished.

"I have a million things on my mind," Jackie said, giving him a look which she hoped appeared aloof.

Mitch gave her a subtle wink. "The thing to do is try and sort them out and then just concentrate on one at a time."

There was no doubt about which one he wanted her to concentrate on first. "Maybe when you get around to playing some music, I'll give it a try."

Mitch grinned and then he blew a few notes. "I honor requests. What would you like to hear?" He ran his fingertips caressingly over the brass keys, lightly tapping each one while he waited for her to reply.

Disturbingly, Jackie's attention slid with his fingers. She thought of him touching her in the same caressing way he was touching his horn and her heart tipped over. Had that been tenderness in his eyes when he had run his fingers through her hair? If this were one of her fantasies she would have wanted to believe it. But this wasn't a fantasy. "You choose." Her green eyes gave nothing away.

"Okay." Mitch slanted his head to her. Thick light-brown hair fell carelessly on his forehead. Shifting his weight a little to one side, he wet his mouth again, sucked in on his horn and started to play. He played "Blue Moon," as she had known he would.

Her senses were immediately assaulted by the intoxicating mixture of the man and his music. Jackie watched the provocative rotation of his mouth. He was impossibly handsome, aggressively virile, and just as aggressively sure of himself. He had every reason to be.

Perspiration beading his upper lip, Mitch played the song through a second time without any stops. He kept his eyes on her, expecting any second to see a dreaminess in her gaze, a flush to her cheeks—the kind of look a woman gives a man when she knows he's romancing her. He was romancing her; making sweet love to her with the song. But if she were at all responsive or affected, she wasn't letting it show. Polite attention was all he could see in her expression. Just as well, Mitch thought with heightening irritation. Hell, what was he doing anyway? If he was smart, he would have his mind on earning his retainer.

Mitch took his lips off the mouthpiece. He let out a breath. "Would you like to hear something else?" he asked brusquely.

She'd had about as much as she could take. How

long could she maintain her feigned indifference? The man and his music were deadly on her nerves. "It's up to you," Jackie answered with contrived casualness.

He really wasn't in the mood to play anymore. But he did. He played a real oldie, something upbeat, one he didn't think she knew. The title of the piece escaped him.

To busy herself, Jackie checked her watch as he finished the song. It took her a second to focus on the time. She knew she should be leaving now to meet the steamboat bringing in her staff. Only, she wasn't sure she could stand.

Mitch unhooked the strap from around his neck and laid his saxophone on the table. "Didn't you like the music?" he asked.

"You already know that I like your music. But that isn't what you're asking, is it?" Jackie got to her feet, giving him a knowing look. Slicing through her tension was a streak of anger.

"What do you think I'm asking about?"

"I know what you are asking about. You want to know whether I reacted to your sexy performance, not the music."

"Sexy?" Mitch asked. The single word question was a direct challenge.

"Oh, you know damn well that you were giving me one of your seduction routines," Jackie retorted.

"Was I?" Mitch gave her a slow, measuring look.

"You were," Jackie stormed. "And you are good! You know all the right moves, even that little wiggle to your hips. Very sexy."

"How good?" Mitch slid an arm around her waist.

70

"Very good," Jackie answered, quickly finding control. "But not good enough."

His eyes met hers. He tightened his arm around her waist. "What is good enough?"

Jackie tried to pull out of his grasp but couldn't. She started to protest but that wasn't the message in her eyes. It was her look that brought his mouth toward her lips. Jackie turned her head sharply away.

Mitch pulled in a deep breath. "What's the matter?"

"I don't want you to kiss me."

"Yes, you do. Just as you wanted me to kiss you yesterday. Only, yesterday you didn't change your mind."

"Yesterday was different," Jackie said, pulling herself free.

He watched her move her hands to her hair, smoothing it back, obviously composing herself. "Why was yesterday different?" He reached over, caught hold of a wayward strand of her honey-blond hair and tucked it behind her ear.

She didn't answer that question. "I really do have to go down to meet the boat. If you want to come along, you can."

"Why was yesterday different?" Mitch questioned again, following her to the back door.

"It just was," Jackie said, walking out as he held it open. Yesterday, she hadn't known what he could make her feel.

"I don't understand." He pushed.

Jackie sent him a speculative look. "You know something? There's a lot about you that I don't understand either."

Mitch slanted her a returning glance. "I guess then

71

that we have a lot of getting to know each other to do." He felt his gut tighten over the thought of what he might find out for sure.

The steamboat had docked. Some of the members of Jackie's staff had already filed off, while the crew from the boat was wheeling cartons on iron dollies down a plank.

Mitch looked downhill at the narrow stretch of sandy beach meeting crystalline blue water. He tried to get his mind clear to concentrate. Dammit! He'd gotten so caught up in sensual visions of Jacqueline Lacey that he'd let his mind drift away from the real reason he was here. Playing with Jackie was playing with fire. Up till now, he'd known how not to get burned. With Jacqueline Lacey, he could get burned in a lot of ways.

Mitch focused in on the people getting off the boat. If Jackie was running a fencing operation someone on her staff could be in it with her. He wished he could talk himself into thinking someone on her staff could be working it alone. Or was he just on the wrong track entirely?

Surprised, Mitch picked out Shannon Grant—the receptionist from Jackie's LA office. She was talking with a couple of the crew men from the boat. According to his check, Shannon Grant had not gone on any of the other fantasy tours. She was strictly based in the office.

"Did you begin without us?" One of three men standing together called out to Jackie. The one who asked was Clayton Brooks, as Mitch found out when Jackie introduced him. "Clayton is our chef on all of our fantasy vacations," she explained. "Mitch started

72

his vacation early. He's been staying over in St. Mary's," she elaborated. Mitch could see in the quick look Jackie threw his way that she was still thinking over his story.

"This is Josh Harris," Jackie continued. "Josh will be playing the part of Merlin for us."

Mitch shook hands with Josh. Mitch knew that playing a role was no novelty for Josh Harris. He was an actor and in between working the fantasies, he hit the studios regularly looking for legitimate acting work. All he had to his credit so far were some TV commercials. In Hollywood, being tall, dark, handsome and having a terrific physique was too common to count.

"Paul Christopher," Jackie said, identifying the last male member of her staff. "Paul is an expert in the martial arts and he has been a bodyguard for some very famous stars."

Paul put an arm around her and whispered something in her ear. Mitch's eyes touched on Paul's hand on Jackie's shoulder and then fixed on her face. He tried to tell himself he didn't care whether or not she had something going with Paul, unless it concerned his investigation. But it was useless to try. He was getting all caught up with her.

"Paul is going to be your instructor in the physical skills necessary for knighthood," Jackie said, smiling after Paul finished whispering to her.

Mitch's eyes stayed a second longer on Jackie's face. She gave him nothing in her look to interpret.

The expression on Paul Christopher's face as he extended his hand to Mitch was not hard to read. Paul

Christopher was sizing him up as possible competition for Jacqueline Lacey.

"I'm looking forward to your instruction," Mitch said after they both had a go at cracking each other's knuckles.

"I'm looking forward to it myself," Paul returned, smoothing his blond hair, not that it needed any smoothing. He wore his hair short, almost in a crew cut. The style added to his boyish appeal. Did he appeal to Jackie? Mitch couldn't say why, but he didn't think so.

"Where are Maggi and Nina?" Jackie asked, looking around.

Paul answered, "Nina got a cut on her arm and Maggi is fixing her up. You know Maggi, she'll probably have Nina bandaged from head to toe."

Jackie smiled. "Maybe I'd better go and see if everything is all right."

"I'll go," Josh said as Shannon Grant came up in her white shorts and skimpy halter top.

"Shannon Grant, Mitch Corey," Jackie said, tightening up as she noted the rather seductive smile Shannon focused on Mitch. Jackie knew Mitch Corey would be noticing it too. And she was certain that he would respond and would most likely redirect his interest from her to Shannon. Or even more likely, he was the kind of guy who could be interested in more than one woman at a time. That was Jacqueline Lacey's opinion of Mitch Corey.

"We've already met," Shannon said, letting Mitch know with her sultry brown eyes that she hadn't forgotten his face and would like to get acquainted with more of him.

74

Mitch smiled. Shannon's provocative approach would have normally sparked his interest but for some reason it was leaving him flat now. He knew what that reason was. Still, he would have played on Shannon's come-on if he thought there was any chance she could be involved with the fencing operation. But he knew that whoever was involved had to be someone who made the trip each time. That seemed to leave Shannon out. "I didn't know that you were going to be on this fantasy tour."

"This is a first for me. Jackie was short-staffed and I volunteered." Shannon made eye contact. "I just know that even though I'm working, I'm going to have a good time."

"I'm sure you will," said Mitch, catching a look at Jackie and seeing an intensity in her green eyes before she walked away.

Mitch caught up with her as she headed for the boat. "No," he said, facing straight ahead.

Jackie turned her eyes on him. "What, no?" she asked, annoyed.

"I'm not interested in Shannon," Mitch clarified.

"You are being presumptuous. I don't care whether you are or you aren't interested in Shannon." Only she *did* care. She would just prefer that he not know it. But how could he miss knowing it? She didn't need a mirror to tell her that her eyes were decidedly greener with jealousy and that her face was all flushed at being caught handing him a bold-faced lie.

Maggi Hart was coming off the boat with Nina Carroll in tow. Jackie waved to them and then rushed forward. Mitch listened to her ask about Nina's cut and he watched her exchange a long affectionate embrace with Maggi. It surprised him to see the ever-reserved Jacqueline Lacey being so demonstrative.

"Maggi Hart and Nina Carroll . . . This is Mitch Corey," Jackie said, taking care of the introductions. "Maggi has been with me from the start. Nina is a music major working with us for the summer."

Mitch had checked out Maggi Hart and she was also on his list as possible suspects, primarily because she had been making these trips from the start. He knew she was widowed and she had grown children. She'd left a selling job at a department store where she'd also doubled as a cosmetician to come work for Jackie. Whatever cosmetics Maggi Hart had been using had stood her in good stead. She looked a lot younger than her age and with her trim, petite figure she could have easily passed for her early forties. According to her driver's license she was fifty-two.

Mitch didn't know anything about Nina Carroll, but she looked exactly like what she was: a college student in a denim skirt and wire-rimmed glasses who'd just stepped off the campus of UCLA. It didn't take any genius on his part to figure out the school. She had the letters ironed on the back of her orange polo shirt.

"I think we'd better get going." Jackie started off with Maggi at her side.

Nina looked around with big innocent hazel eyes and watched Josh, Clayton, and Paul lead the crew from the boat with the cartons.

"What instrument do you play?" Mitch asked, walking with Nina. His eyes followed Jackie.

"Harp, cello, and violin. There's a harp in one of the cartons." Nina continued to look wide-eyed in her

76

wire-rimmed frames. "Have you seen the castle yet?" she asked.

"Yes. And if you look through those trees over there you'll be able to get a glimpse of it."

Nina craned her neck as they continued walking. "I think I do see it. Oh, my gosh! It *is* a castle!"

She was on the plump side—too old for it to be called baby fat anymore. And she had a rather plain-looking face, but the glow of excitement that flushed her cheeks made her almost pretty. Mitch smiled at her and tried to remember if he'd ever been able to look at the world through rose-colored glasses. There probably was a time, but he couldn't remember back that far.

Once inside the castle, Nina went off with Jackie, Shannon, and Maggi. Mitch followed after Paul, Josh, and Clayton, who in turn followed the crew from the boat wheeling in the cartons. Clayton excused himself, saying he was going to see to preparing some brunch, and Paul and Josh began lifting the cartons.

"Tell me where these go and I'll give you a hand," Mitch offered.

Josh answered, "I don't think Jackie would like the idea of putting one of the guests to work."

Paul said, "What's the big deal? If he wants to give us a hand, let him." Paul pointed to one of the cartons. "That one goes to your chamber. I'll show you the way."

"I know the way," Mitch replied, lifting the carton that Paul had pointed out.

"Just how early did you arrive?" Paul asked, annoyed.

"Early enough," Mitch answered, giving Paul a solemn wink to interpret before he headed for the stairs.

Mitch looked through the carton when he was in his chamber. As he expected, it contained a suit of armor and other clothing of a knight. Tired, he stretched out on the bed for a while. What was he going to do about her? What was he going to do about himself?

"I was just going to send someone to look for you," Jackie said as Mitch walked into the kitchen. The whole group were seated at the table. Jackie and Maggi were helping Clayton prepare brunch.

Mitch walked up to Jackie. She was standing at one of the counters, adding some sprigs of parsley to a platter of cold cuts.

"That looks good," Mitch said, glancing down.

His nearness made her feel awkward and shaky in an instant. "Could you carry this to the table for me?" She wanted him to move away from her.

"Sure," Mitch answered, lifting the platter off the counter. Jackie eased herself past him and crossed the room. Clayton followed Mitch to the table with a tray of deviled eggs.

"I understand that's your saxophone," Shannon said, smiling to Mitch as he laid the cold cuts on the table.

Mitch noticed his saxophone now over on one of the counters where Jackie must have carefully placed it on a couple of towels. He'd forgotten he'd left it in the kitchen but he hadn't forgotten playing for her.

"Yes, it is," Mitch answered, sliding a glance over at Jackie as she sat down between Paul and Josh. He sat down next to Shannon.

"I love the saxophone." Shannon smiled. "I hope I can talk you into playing for me."

"I understand that you have a club in Hollywood," Josh said, speaking from across the table.

"Yes," Mitch replied smoothly.

Maggi and Clayton came to the table and sat down. Maggi brought the ice tea. Clayton laid down a wicker basket of bread and rolls.

Jackie asked, "Paul, after lunch I want you to take the motorboat and follow Mitch back to St. Mary's so that he can turn in the one he rented from there." She wanted Mitch Corey out of her hair for a while. Even with her staff around, his nearness was producing a most unsettling effect on her. No man had ever reached her in the way he did. He made her feel a sensuality inside that she hadn't even known existed. That awareness was frightening to her—but it was also exciting.

Mitch accepted the platter of cold cuts as it was passed around the table. He helped himself to a few slices of ham and took a roll.

"Won't you need me to help you here? The helicopter will be arriving with everyone in a couple of hours," Paul said, arguing.

"We'll manage to get everything set up," Jackie answered firmly.

For endless seconds, no one at the table spoke. Jackie could feel Mitch's eyes on her. She wondered if he was picking up on her tension.

Nina exclaimed, "I can't wait to put on a costume."

"I hope you'll like the ones I chose for you." Jackie smiled, grateful to have a conversation going.

"Oh, I know I will," Nina gushed.

"There's a pink gown that is going to look especially good with your coloring. I knew it was right for you the minute I saw it," Jackie said sincerely.

Shannon said, "I'm glad that I went along with you and picked out my own costumes. There's a red gown that I'm crazy about."

Offering her cosmetic expertise, Maggi said, "It's been my experience that redheads don't usually look good in red." Shannon had straight bright auburn hair that was cut blunt at her shoulders.

Before Shannon had a chance to answer, Clayton intruded on the conversation and changed the subject. "Jackie, I hope you got all the spices and herbs that I had on my list."

"You always worry, Clayton, that I won't get everything and I usually do," Jackie answered patiently.

"You didn't the last trip," Clayton reminded her and then elaborated for Mitch. "Imagine being in Paris, doing a Louis the Fourteenth fantasy and not having any truffles. I was right in the middle of creating one of my most masterful recipes and I looked for the truffles and there weren't any. I've been cooking professionally for fifteen years, mind you, and it's the first time I can remember that I just threw up my hands."

"I was extra careful this time," Jackie said. "I know how hard you work to make everything perfect."

Maggi and Paul shared a grin with each other knowing that wasn't the only time Clayton had thrown up his hands. He threw up his hands at least once during every fantasy.

Clayton continued complaining while everyone else ate.

80

Clayton Brooks was forty-three years old and he had a police record. Mitch knew about it. Clayton had gotten himself picked up on an assault and battery charge when he was in his twenties and hanging around with a fast crowd. He'd served nine months in a county jail in Baltimore. Clayton hadn't added to his police blotter since then but Mitch couldn't dismiss Clayton Brooks as a possible suspect. Still, Mitch doubted that anyone as hot-headed as Clayton Brooks would be controlled enough to deal in cool ice.

When the meal was over, Jackie hustled everyone into action. On the way out of the kitchen with Paul, Mitch noticed Josh taking Shannon aside. They huddled for a minute. From the expression on Shannon's face, Mitch decided she didn't like what Josh had to say.

Mitch stepped outside with Paul and they headed toward the dock. "How long have you been working for Jackie?" Mitch asked, knowing the answer.

"About a year and a half," Paul replied, giving Mitch a fast glance. "You don't seem the type that would go for these fantasy tours. They're a bit sedate. I would think that someone like you would be looking for a little more action."

"What kind of action?" Mitch asked matter-of-factly, aware of what Paul meant.

Paul laughed. "Let me put it this way, man. You'll be wasting your time if you're thinking of making a move on Jacqueline Lacey."

Mitch flashed Paul a sideways look. "Is that a warning?"

"Just a little friendly advice. I speak from experience." Paul shrugged. "A lot of guys fall in love with her on these fantasies. Some even get it in their heads that the way they see her is the way she really is. Jackie can really get carried away when she's playing a role."

Mitch stopped walking, calling a halt to Paul's stride. "What exactly does that mean?"

"It means that when the fantasy is over and Jacqueline Lacey isn't playing a part, she goes back to being hard as nails."

CHAPTER FIVE

The guests had all arrived by the time Mitch and Paul got back from St. Mary's. They were all milling around in the main hall of the castle. Mitch looked around for Jackie. Not seeing her, he tagged Nina as she walked by. "Do you know where Jackie is?"

"She's not here. You see, Clayton had a fit in the kitchen because he couldn't find mint leaves. Jackie insisted that he had not written mint leaves down on his list. Anyway, Jackie remembered that there was a whole patch of mint leaves growing wild somewhere or other and she rode off a little while ago to pick some for Clayton."

Maggi Hart came up. "Nina, would you give me a hand getting the rest of the platters of fruit up to the rooms?"

"Sure," Nina answered, taking off with Maggi.

Around him the fantasy that was to officially begin in the evening was the topic of conversation. A fair-haired guy and a tall leggy brunette introduced themselves to Mitch saying, "This is going to be great fun." Mitch smiled. But Mitch Corey was not having any fun. He was chasing around in circles after a honey blond with green eyes who had larceny on her mind and a block of ice where her heart was supposed to be. She'd said it herself: Money was her passion. Money was her motivation. Couple motivation with opportunity and you come up with a nice, neat package. Transporting jewels under the guise of props made a helluva opportunity. Still, Mitch kept the doubt alive. He supposed that he was forcing it some.

Josh tapped his shoulder. "I'm going to be taking everyone on a tour through the castle. Would you like to come along?"

"I think I'll just take a walk around outside," Mitch responded restlessly.

Walking took him to the stable. He went inside and saddled himself a chestnut bay horse. Mitch rode out wondering which direction Jackie had taken. He had made up his mind to take a new direction with her. From now on, he was going to keep his mind totally on business.

The mint leaves were where she'd remembered seeing them on the last King Arthur fantasy. Jackie picked bunches and stuffed them into the long pockets of her yellow cotton skirt. Mumbling to herself in annoyance about why she was constantly putting up with Clayton's dramatics, Jackie got back up on her horse.

Just as she was grabbing for the reins, a snake curled in the path of the stallion's hoofs. Spooked, the stallion reared.

Somewhere off in the distance, Mitch heard a woman scream and then scream again. He couldn't see her, but he knew it was Jackie. Forcing the bay into a full gallop, Mitch took off.

Rock and dirt were sent flying by the driving, bolting hoofs of her stallion. Mitch could see her leaning far forward in her saddle making a desperate attempt to catch the flapping reins.

Mitch dug his heels in. Riding hard at an angle, he tried to cut her horse off. His heart pounded furiously. "Hold on, Jackie. I'm coming."

Her stallion plunged forward and reared back to plunge forward again as the chestnut bay came close. Mitch could see that there wasn't any way that the stallion was going to allow the bay to cut him off. Pulse racing, Mitch maneuvered to get near enough alongside of her. His eyes quickly assessed the situation as he got close.

"Jackie, kick your feet free of the stirrups," Mitch instructed loudly. He was sure that she saw him and that she heard him but she was panicked. He wasn't far off from panic himself.

The stallion reared again and then changed direction. Mitch fought with the bay to catch up.

"Jackie, kick your feet free of the stirrups . . . Come on Jackie," Mitch pleaded, getting near enough to reach for her.

"Mitch!" Jackie turned wide, frightened green eyes to him. Her fingers were curled tight now in the stallion's mane. Her feet were still in the stirrups. She couldn't seem to make herself move.

"Kick your feet free," Mitch commanded. "Come on, baby. You can do it. I won't let anything happen to you."

Jackie felt Mitch's arm and hand gripping her around the waist, pulling. She went flying through the air, hauled up over his shoulder before he set her in the saddle with him.

Wanting to continue to give the stallion chase, the

chestnut bay bucked under the two of them as Mitch tried to exert control. "Hold on to me, Jackie. I have to use both my hands."

Jackie locked her arms around his neck and clung.

Using both his hands now, Mitch finally brought his horse sliding to a halt in the sand. They'd ridden onto the beach.

Mitch sat for a minute catching his breath and then he swung his foot over the saddle, cradling Jackie in the vee of his legs. "I'm going to bring us both off. Keep your arms around me." Her hands tight around his neck, his hands tight at her waist, Mitch dropped off from the horse, sliding Jackie down in front of him.

She quivered against him as soon as he had her on her feet. He immediately lifted her up in his arms and walked with her away from the sandy beach to the shade of some trees. She winced as he laid her down in the tall grass.

He bent over her anxiously. "Jackie, where does it hurt?"

"I don't know . . . It's okay now." Jackie shifted slightly to settle herself more comfortably and then froze as Mitch began fingering her rib cage. "Stop," she snapped, flapping her hands nervously.

Mitch rested back on his heels, stilling his fingers. "I want to find out where you are hurt," he explained insistently.

"I'm not hurt there," Jackie said, her breathing rushed.

"Where do you think you might be hurt?" His own breathing was a little uneven though he hadn't thought of himself as touching her in any intimate way until she made an issue of it.

Jackie gave him one of her cool, controlled looks. "I'm not hurt there," she said. "I think it's my shoulder."

Mitch returned a teasing smile. "Brace yourself," he said before his fingers moved down to dance slowly across her shoulders.

"I don't need to brace myself," Jackie said, low and angry. "You don't affect me in any way." At the moment, his fingers were playing havoc with her senses. She monitored his face, wondering if he felt any reaction. Nothing in his expression indicated that he did.

When he found a tender area on her right shoulder, Jackie gave a low cry.

Mitch took his fingers off the spot. "I'm just going to rotate your shoulder a little," he said after her features relaxed. "Does this hurt?"

Jackie shook her head. "No."

Mitch rested back on his heels. "I'm sure it's just a bruise."

She saw a flicker of perturbance in his eyes. "What's the matter?" she asked.

He was wondering if he might have hurt her himself when he'd pulled her so hard to him. "I think I should get a cold compress on you," he answered. "I'm going to wet my handkerchief down at the water."

Jackie turned her head, watching him walk. "I'm not very good at saying thank you," she called out to him.

Mitch stopped and looked back at her.

Her heart was clammering. Do you know how close you come to acting out my fantasies? "Thank you for rescuing me," she said, a catch in her voice.

"Isn't that what a knight is supposed to do—rescue the fair damsel in distress?"

"Yes." Jackie sighed, making herself sit up, turning her head from him as she did. The yellow scarf she'd worn to tie her hair back fell off. Unconsciously, she shifted her fingers through the waterfall of golden silk strands.

He stood studying her a second longer with her unaware of his regard. Her eyes had caught on a butterfly. Mitch saw a flash of delight cross her profile. He wished he knew why she rarely let herself show her feelings. Except for brief intermittent moments, a mask of coolness hid her thoughts.

Mitch walked down to the water. When he was there, he splashed his face before he wet his handkerchief and came back to her.

"Here, slip this in under your blouse." He handed her his folded wet handkerchief.

"Hold it a minute." Jackie opened the top two buttons on her yellow embroidered blouse.

Mitch watched her drop the blouse off her bad shoulder, sliding a white bra strap down with it. He sat down on the grass facing her.

"Am I black and blue?" Jackie asked, trying to see for herself.

"No." Mitch cleared his throat against a thickness that he felt there. Did she know how provocative she looked? He knew how much his body wanted her. But not his mind. His mind didn't want her at all.

Jackie took the wet compress from him and held it to her sore shoulder. She slanted her head to the left, sending her hair shimmering down one side. The sun played with each strand.

Mitch fished in the pocket of his slacks for a pack of cigarettes and a lighter. Cupping his hand over the flame, he lit one up. "Did you find the mint leaves?" He watched the lazy rings of smoke he was making with his mouth. He didn't want to lapse into any silences with her.

"Yes." Jackie reached into one of her skirt pockets with her free hand. She took out a bunch of leaves. "How did you know about the mint leaves?"

"Nina mentioned it." He pulled in another deep drag and let it out slowly.

"Have you ever chewed a mint leaf?" She studied him as she asked. His light-brown hair was askew from the hard ride and she knew that was the way he would look first thing in the morning. An undefined sensation spread slowly through her.

"No, I don't think so."

Jackie bent forward and brushed a leaf across his lips. "Here, taste one."

Mitch took it from her and put it in his mouth. "Why did you say that you are not good at saying thank you?" he asked her suddenly.

"I don't know."

Mitch Corey's blue eyes rested on her face. "What makes you so afraid to let anyone get close to you?" He shot the question at her and watched her stiffen.

"I don't know what you mean." Her tone was defensive. He had already gotten closer to her than she wanted him to be.

Mitch ground out his cigarette in the grass, deciding at the same time to drop the subject. What was the point in trying to know anything about her? There was only one thing he needed to find out. "Let me have a

89

look at your shoulder." He reached forward to take his handkerchief from her and then he leaned in front of her to check her bruise. He was very close.

Jackie felt her pulse trip. His mouth was so near to hers. A hidden tremor shivered through her body. She waited for him to kiss her, wanting him to. But he made no attempt.

Mitch blew a breath against her lips. "It's up to you," he whispered.

She didn't want it to be up to her, she wanted to be able to disclaim the kiss afterward. But try as she might, she could not resist the desire to feel his mouth over hers. Jackie moved her lips softly across his, expecting him to take control as she conceded. When he didn't, Jackie drew back, feeling confused, tremulous, and angry. She pushed his hand aside and held his handkerchief to her shoulder.

"Change your mind again?" Mitch asked, flattening his hands at either side of her legs. A pulse raced along his throat.

Jackie heard a taunt in his voice and saw it reflected in his gaze. Her eyes frosted over. "I think we should get back to the castle." She tossed his handkerchief on the grass.

"Okay." Mitch continued to lean toward her.

Watching him, Jackie seductively raised her bra strap, then she slowly buttoned her blouse. She knew from his eyes that she was enticing him now. She meant to.

"Is that an invitation or just another tease?" Mitch asked laconically.

"Neither," Jackie retorted, finding herself annoyed

with her behavior. Or was she just annoyed with his response?

"If you'll move, I'd like to get up." When he didn't move, Jackie brought her hands up to his chest to push him back. It was then that something other than Mitch Corey dented her consciousness. "My ring," she exclaimed. "I've lost my ring."

Mitch let out a deep breath that he hadn't realized he'd been holding. "What kind of ring?"

"An emerald ring." Jackie dug her fingers through the grass as he moved back.

Automatically and instinctively, Mitch thought of the insurance company pictures that he'd brought with him of the latest jewelry heisted in LA. He screened through them in his mind while he helped her look. He couldn't recall seeing an emerald ring and he was good at recall.

"I'll go over and look on the beach," he said. "It might have come loose when I took you off the horse. Is it real?" he asked.

"Yes, it's very real and very expensive. I have to find it," Jackie rambled miserably as her fingers tore through the grass around her.

The hoofs of the chestnut bay were still imprinted clearly in the sand. The bay had moseyed over to dine on a currant berry bush. Mitch sifted around through the sand. An expensive emerald ring brought up other issues in his mind . . . He was tense all over again.

After ten minutes or so, Mitch turned up the ring. "I found it," he shouted out to her.

She came running.

Mitch wiped it clean with his fingers and then held

it up to the sun to look at it. The stone was the exact shade of green as her eyes. "Gift?" he asked flippantly.

"Yes." Jackie extended her hand to take it.

Mitch palmed it, closing his fist. He thought about her with Vic Logan. The old man could well afford to give her expensive gifts. He'd just bet that she knew how to say thank you well enough for a ring like this. His features hardened. "Who gave it to you?"

"That is none of your business," Jackie answered.

His cynical gaze studied her defiant expression. "I know," Mitch drawled dryly. "You've got yourself a nice sugar daddy." The ring was burning a hole in his hand.

Jackie glared at him.

He glared back at her. "I guess jewelry like this brings out your passion a lot faster than sweet music."

Jackie reeled at his insult and then she hauled off to slap his face. Mitch quickly gripped her wrist, stopping her. "You'll hurt your shoulder worse. Who gave you this ring?" he demanded.

Her eyes blazed with green fire. "I bought the ring for myself. Are you satisfied?" she asked furiously.

He reeled back a little himself as he let go of her wrist.

"Do you expect me to believe that you bought this for yourself?" He wasn't sure whether or not to believe her, but if she did buy it, then where did she get the money? One answer shot into his mind. Fencing jewels is a very profitable business.

"I don't care what you believe," Jackie said angrily. "Just give it to me."

His eyes not any less angry than hers, Mitch opened his hand. She grabbed her ring.

"I know you are doing pretty well with these tours, but you still don't make enough money to buy yourself a trinket like this."

Jackie pushed the ring down on her finger. "How do you know what I earn?" she asked and then barreled along. "I didn't earn it the way you are thinking. I saved up for it because I wanted it. I don't need any man to give me anything."

Mitch watched her chin come up and her shoulders straighten. She turned on her heels and walked over to the chestnut bay. He reached her at the horse and placed his hands on her waist, stopping her from trying to mount on her own. He climbed into the saddle and then swung down and raised her up. He settled her sideways in front of him.

She sat staring ahead, moodily hugging her arms together.

Mitch took her hands apart and placed one around his back. "I've told you that I want you to hold on to me when we ride."

Jackie stuck her nails into his shirt, meaning to hurt. "You know," she said, giving him a hastily contrived indifferent look. "You would have done well in King Arthur's time. You seem to enjoy the role of a knight having a lady lean on you."

Mitch kicked the bay into action. "And you don't lean . . ." he said for her. "Then what role will you play when the fantasy begins?"

"You'll find out," Jackie answered with a cool, crisp bite to her voice.

She wore a white gown with flowing sleeves that left her shoulders bare. A silver girdle hugged her narrow waist and then dipped low to one side. Her hair shimmered like molten gold as it caught the light of the tapers in the great hall. That light seemed centered on her, giving her an incandescent beauty. Even from across the room, she took his breath away.

Everyone was in costume. Couples were dancing while Nina played a harp. The combination of sound had a haunting quality.

A hauberk concealed much of his heavily embroidered long-sleeved gipon shirt. Both garments—the shirt and the vest—reached to just below his knees. He wore maille chausses that were laced up his legs. Waistchains that sheathed a small dagger closed around his masculine hips. Even as she spoke with others, she saw him the minute he came in. He was the knight of her fantasies. Only this fantasy was becoming too real for her to handle.

Mitch started toward her, passing on the way a granite round table laden with food and drink. He noticed it only briefly. His eyes were on her. Jacqueline was mesmerizing and his were not the only male eyes held captive by her.

Merlin stepped in front of Mitch, detaining him. "Ah, Sir Lancelot," Josh said, assigning Mitch a role for the evening's festivities as he had done with each of the guests. "I welcome your return to King Arthur's court."

"Sir Lancelot?" Mitch asked, looking Josh over. If he hadn't known it was Josh playing the role of Merlin, Mitch would have had difficulty recognizing him. Josh wore a white-haired wig, a white-haired long beard, a black-hooded robe, and a cone-shaped black hat.

"So, Sir Lancelot, how did the latest battle go?" Merlin inquired.

"The battle went well, Merlin," Mitch answered, playing along.

"We wouldn't expect less from the bravest knight of the Round Table." Merlin smiled.

Mitch looked from Josh to again scan the room for Jackie. He saw her talking now with Paul, who was also dressed as a knight.

"Would you like me to present you to the Lady Nimue?" Merlin asked, following the direction of Mitch's gaze.

"Yes." Mitch knew that Josh meant Jackie.

"I first must warn you, Sir Lancelot, that she is a most powerful enchantress—a sorceress whose magic is the strongest of any woman you will ever come to know."

The role of an enchantress was exactly right for her, Mitch thought. "Tell me, Merlin, is there no spell that can break the enchantress's power?"

"No, Sir Lancelot. Merlin can do many things, but not even Merlin can silence an enchantress's song."

"What if the knight wishes to listen to the song?" Mitch asked, thinking the melody had begun the first time he saw her.

"The knight can only answer that question for himself." Josh wondered just how much was going on between Mitch Corey and Jacqueline Lacey.

Jackie could hear herself talking too much, smiling too much, struggling hard not to look anywhere but directly at Paul. She was cognizant of Mitch and Josh walking toward her and she was instantly aware when Mitch had reached her side. Her breath thinned and she could do no more than nod her head to Paul as he finished off saying something that she had not absorbed.

Josh cleared his throat. "May I present Sir Lancelot to you, my lady."

Green eyes that were still angry met blue eyes that stayed cool.

"My lady," Mitch said, taking her hand and bringing it to his lips.

"Sir Lancelot." Jackie took her hand away from him.

But when she would have left, he stopped her.

"Will you dance with me, my lady?" He could see in her eyes that she was going to refuse and so he quickly fired his arm around her waist. He listened to her refusal as he dragged her away to the dance floor.

"I said that I don't want to dance with you," Jackie repeated tightly as he turned her into his arms.

Mitch planted both his hands on the small of her back, bringing the length of her body against his. "How's your shoulder?"

"Fine." Jackie kept her hands down at her sides. "Will you please stop. I don't want to dance with you."

"I'm not going to let you go until the song ends." Mitch smiled at her easily. "I'm sure you don't want to make a scene and spoil the fantasy for everyone here. Why don't you just put your arms up around my neck and make the best of it."

Jackie brought her hands up to the front of his shoulders, making space between them.

Mitch guided one hand of hers at a time up and

around his neck. "What is that lovely fragrance you're wearing?" he asked softly.

"Heather." She thought to move her hands back down to his shoulders but she didn't.

"Heather," Mitch said and then didn't say anything more.

Jackie found that not only her body drifted with his but that her mind drifted also as they moved rhythmically together.

Mitch felt her warm, sweet breath against the side of his neck. Jackie felt his breath across her temple. He touched the silkiness of her hair. She moved her hands across the width of his broad shoulders and then back around his neck. She had her eyes closed. For a moment, so did he.

The song ended but he didn't let her go. She didn't realize until seconds later that there was no longer any music.

Jackie pulled away, feeling flustered though she didn't let it show. She could see that everyone had taken seats at the table, which meant that Josh had announced that the feasting was to begin. Only she'd been too wrapped up in Mitch Corey to hear Josh.

Mitch took her hand and led her to the table. He pulled out a chair for her, taking the one next to her for himself. She refused to look at him. He refused to let himself think that later he would leave her here to search her chamber.

Merlin stood. "Noble knights of the Round Table, cut from these meats with your blades and serve yourselves and these fair ladies. Eat and be merry. After the feast, I shall tell you tales of King Arthur's court and entertain you with magic."

Mitch took out the blade sheathed in his waist-chains as did all the other knights. On the table there were chickens and fish left whole, along with sides of beef in quarters. There were vegetables in bunches, assortments of breads, and silver pitchers of red ruby wine. "What would you like, fair lady?" Mitch asked Jackie.

"Some chicken and some broccoli."

Mitch cut slices for her until she stopped him. Then he served himself a cut of beef. He filled both of their goblets with wine. She ate, drinking only a little. He drank more than he ate.

Jackie slanted a glance at him. "Don't you like eating with your hands?"

"I'm not too hungry." He had a sinking feeling in the pit of his stomach. He couldn't stop thinking about later searching her room.

"Are you feeling all right?" Jackie asked.

"Just a little tired. I think I'm going to make it an early night." Mitch avoided her eyes. He watched Maggi, Nina, and Clayton clear the table and set out wet cloths.

Before the desserts were served, Merlin got to his feet. "Tonight's tale is one of Sir Lancelot and the Lady of the Lake," Josh began and then paused for attention before he continued. "It came to pass that one day Sir Lancelot rode off from Camelot in quest of a golden eagle to please Queen Guinevere who had sent him forth. As he rode through the forests seeking the bird, he came across a wondrous sight. For there was a lake whose waters were the bluest he had ever seen and rising from the lake was a maiden of extraordinary beauty. Because of her appearance and the look about her, he was aware that she was not like any other woman but was doubtless enchantment." Merlin walked around the table, stopping behind Jackie and Mitch.

Jackie sat wishing Josh had chosen a different tale for tonight. She felt as if she were being caught up in a real fantasy inside of a pretend fantasy and she didn't want to be caught up in anything that she didn't control.

Juxtaposed over Josh's story, Mitch saw a picture of Jackie the way he had found her at the lake and he found himself suddenly wanting to hightail it out of here. Was she truly enchantment?

"Rise, Lady Nimue and Sir Lancelot. For we will have you show us how the tale unfolds," Josh said.

Mitch got to his feet first and then helped Jackie from her chair. She sought out his gaze but his look was too complicated and she couldn't read at all what he was thinking.

Merlin stood to the side of the players. "Sir Lancelot approached the Lady of the Lake and then he knelt down before her." Josh motioned with his hand for Mitch to do so.

Mitch knelt down before Jackie. A vein throbbed at his temple as his glance lifted to hers.

She thought to lose herself in her part, making it only an act. The words came out but she was too on edge to find the right feeling. "Why dost thou kneel to me?" she asked falteringly.

Josh started to speak, prompting Mitch, but Mitch was already answering.

"You are incredibly beautiful," he said as if the words were being pulled out of him and he had no choice but to say them. "I kneel because you are enchantment." He held her eyes.

Jackie broke away from his look. She was trembling inside. What was he doing to her? "Kneel no longer, Sir Lancelot. For you are a most wondrous knight."

Merlin said, "Sir Lancelot beheld the magical qualities of the lady. He perceived that her skin was ivory and that her eyes were green like emeralds and that her hair was long and perfectly fair. He perceived that she had about her neck necklaces of opals and emeralds set in gold and that about her wrists were bracelets of finely wrought silver."

Mitch's eyes stayed on her. Jackie's eyes stayed away from his.

Merlin narrated. "After Sir Lancelot had studied her long and hard, he asked for her name."

"Who are you?" Mitch asked intently.

"An enchantress," Jackie answered, looking into his face to find his features as intense as his voice.

"What power does the enchantress have?" His intensity remained.

"I have the power to cast you a spell," Jackie responded, not hearing that she, too, had become intense.

Josh looked from Jackie to Mitch. He could be projecting but it seemed to him there were sparks of a battle going on between them. Then Josh spoke, picking up from where he had left off. "And so saying, the Lady Nimue took from around her neck the long necklace of opals and emeralds that she wore."

Jackie took off from around her neck a chain of fake opals and emeralds. She moved toward Mitch. "Wear this, Sir Knight," she said, offering it to him. "It is of very potent magic. It will give to you the same power as mine."

And then Merlin said, "Having given Sir Lancelot her necklace, the Lady turned and vanished."

Mitch watched Jackie walk away. He saw her say something to Paul and then exit the great hall.

"Sir Lancelot stood like one in a dream," Merlin said. "For he was not sure if what he had beheld was only a vision. But he knew when he placed the necklace on, that what he felt was an enchantment." And so saying, Merlin took off his cone-shaped hat and bowed to those who sat at the Round Table.

Mitch stood holding the necklace in his hand, waiting for her to reappear. He felt as if she had stepped out of a dream. Or had he stepped into a dream with her?

Mitch saw Josh go back to the table and sit down, but still Jackie did not return. Mitch flashed a look at Paul and then he went over to ask him about Jackie.

"She retired for the evening," Paul answered. "I guess she must have gotten tired of your company."

Mitch stared at her necklace. He didn't know it then but he was to see Jacqueline Lacey before the night ended. Destiny was to take a hand.

CHAPTER SIX

Mitch stood on the parapet outside his chamber and smoked the last cigarette in a pack he'd bought over a week ago. He took a final deep satisfying drag and then stamped the butt out with the heel of his sneaker. He'd traded his knight's attire for Levi's and a short-sleeved blue chambray shirt that he hadn't bothered to button. Neither had he bothered to try to sleep. He was feeling very tense.

The castle was quiet. He made his way along the parapet and then down the candlelit stairs. Once outside, Mitch headed for the stable.

The stable wasn't locked. Mitch hitched a saddle on a white stallion. He mounted the horse and rode off into the earliest moment of dawn.

Jackie came out of the Pool of Pendragon shivering from her swim. The air, permeated with the scent of wild heather, promised the warmth of day but the water had been almost ice cold. She towel-dried her hair and her body. Then she dressed, putting on her bikini panties first and then the pink costume gown she had slept in. She tied a silver braid at her waist and bent for her sandals. As she did, she thought she heard the sound of brush crackling not very far away. Forgetting about her sandals, Jackie looked around. It was then that she saw the dim outline of a horse and rider advancing.

At first she couldn't make out who rode the white stallion. Then she did and it wasn't any phantom out of her imagination. This phantom was very clear and vivid.

He saw her immediately. His first thought was to be smart and turn the stallion back in the direction of the castle without making any stops. But then, since he'd met her, he had forgotten how to be smart.

Jackie watched him rein in the white stallion next to her horse. He dismounted agilely and walked toward her. She drew in a deep breath. She didn't know it but so did he.

"What are you doing here?" she asked in a strained voice.

"I couldn't sleep. I guess you couldn't either." He took her in with his eyes. She'd been swimming. Her hair tumbled wet down the back of her high-necked costume. The bodice clung damply to her. Mitch Corey started making promises to himself that he knew he couldn't keep.

"I wouldn't have thought that you would have remembered the way here." She fidgeted first with her hair and then with the bodice of her gown. She pinched tucks down the front trying to ease the material away from her nipples.

Mitch tore his eyes up from what she was doing to her face. It was light enough for him to see his own tension mirrored in her expression. "The horse seemed to be guided on its own. Perhaps it was fate that led the way."

"Fate?" Her voice sounded hoarse and unnatural, when she'd meant it to be scornful and mocking.

"Don't you believe in fate?"

"No," Jackie answered quickly.

Her eyes met his. His asked another question. Hers pleaded with him not to put it in words. Two hearts beat faster. Both knew the words didn't matter.

"I suppose you don't believe in destiny either . . ." He looked at her and tried to find some hard resolve left. He tried but there wasn't any.

"No." Her breath caught as she watched him raise his hand. But he didn't make any attempt to touch her. Instead he kneaded the back of his neck, massaging the corded muscles there. She knew that he had seen her tremble.

"I happen to believe in fate and in destiny," Mitch said after a moment. He thought of himself as stalking her, but for a second there, he'd wondered which one of them really was the prey. But there were two things he was certain about: He couldn't stay away from her and he couldn't let her go.

"I suppose you know what *your* destiny is." Even as she spoke she could hear her own pulse in her ears.

"I know *our* destiny. Just as you do." He took a step toward her.

"I don't intend to live out some crazy fantasy between you and me. Do you understand?" Jackie cried.

"Perfectly," Mitch answered, pulling her to him.

Jackie splayed her hands against his upper arms. His biceps hardened at her touch. "It's just a fantasy. It's not real," she said, lying to him because she was afraid in a way she didn't know how to explain.

Mitch's gaze flickered over her face and then became hooded, obstructing her from reading anything in his eyes. He felt a slashing pain in his head. But it was also his wish not to make it real. Real was love. He didn't want it to be anything more than just sex. Since his divorce, sex had replaced love. He'd had sex with brunettes, blondes, and redheads. He'd had good sex. He'd had sex for the sake of having sex. Sometimes he had sex with the same woman more than once. Most times he didn't. Most times he didn't even remember their names. Most times he didn't think that they remembered his.

"Is it just a fantasy?" Mitch asked, wishing desperately that it was, knowing with the same desperation that it wasn't.

The question floated around her. She was no longer thinking of evading the truth. She pressed her mouth to his trying to answer him. The answer was in her need for his kiss, his touch. The answer was deep in her heart. The answer was his for the asking.

His arm stayed loose around her waist while his mouth only just met the slow, seductive movement of hers. He offered nothing but that didn't lessen the feeling of wantonness that she was experiencing for the very first time.

She slid her hands inside his opened shirt exploring his hard, warm flesh, snapping his control until he was kissing her so hard that he was bruising her lips. But she wouldn't have stopped him. He stopped himself, sharply jerking his head back.

Jackie sagged against him, supporting herself to his strength. Her head dropped to his shoulder.

Mitch shakily meshed his fingers through her hair.

"It isn't a fantasy for me," he whispered in a strangled voice. "Not a fantasy . . ."

Jackie lifted her head. His eyes immediately connected with hers, then crawled down to her mouth all swollen from the way he had just kissed her.

"I think I'm falling in love with you," Jackie confessed. "I don't want to be in love with you. I don't want to be in love at all."

He couldn't seem to take his next breath. The hard core of Mitch Corey was shattering, leaving him lost on unfamiliar ground. He wasn't sure what to do. The words were there in his head—*I've already fallen in love with you*—but he couldn't say them.

Jackie looked up at him, her eyes wide and bright. He touched her bruised lips softly with his thumb. "Give me your mouth. I'll make it better."

Jackie brought her arms up around his neck and closed her eyes. Mitch outlined her lips lightly with his tongue. He stroked her mouth tenderly with his, moving his hands up under the long spill of her hair. And she honored him back with the sweetest kiss he'd ever had, reawakening parts of him that had functioned meaninglessly for years.

She skimmed his teeth with her tongue and then caressed his mouth with hers. She felt dreamy and she wanted to hold on to that feeling. Hands on her hips moved her more fully in place. She could feel him hard and aroused. Involuntarily, she stiffened.

Mitch felt the stiffness all through her. Jackie slid her hips away, wedging a space between them. Mitch stood perfectly still. Pulse racing in confusion, he kissed her mouth softly and then eased his lips away.

His eyes searched her face. "Do you want me to stop?"

Jackie turned out of his embrace. "I want you to make love to me. It's just that I'm not very good at this. I might disappoint you."

A long second went by with Mitch trying to absorb what she was saying. "Do you think that you could disappoint me?" he asked, incredulous.

"I'm not very passionate." Jackie looked at him with huge luminous green eyes.

He had seen the pride of Jacqueline Lacey. He had seen her defiance. But he had never seen any of her insecurity or hurt.

"Did your ex-husband tell you that you disappointed him?" Mitch's voice was low with shock. How could any man who had held her and kissed her and made love to her have been disappointed?

"Yes," Jackie answered unwaveringly.

Mitch gathered her back into the circle of his arms. He raised her chin. "Jackie, your ex-husband must have been a fool." He gave her a soft smile. "I'm sure other men must have told you . . ." Disconcerted by the look in her eyes, he abruptly cut himself off.

She waited for him to ask the question. He didn't. She answered him anyway. "I haven't had any other lovers."

She blew his mind—what was left of it. Mitch closed his eyes briefly and then opened them to focus on her again. "No one else?" he asked in a raw voice.

"No." She shook her head. "I'm afraid of you, afraid of what you can make me feel. I wish I could stop myself from wanting you."

"Don't be afraid, baby. Don't be afraid," Mitch

107

groaned through a chain of kisses—none reaching even a measure of his fire. He had no idea how to be with her.

He lifted her hair off her neck, and ran his tongue along the line of her throat. He touched her a little with his hands where he most wanted to touch her a lot.

A slick film covered his temple. Denim stretched taut over masculine contours.

"Mitch," Jackie moaned. She couldn't get anything else to come out. In a wonderful daze, she took hold of his hands when he went to take them off her breasts and kept them there.

"Do you want me to touch you more?" His voice was husky.

"Yes," Jackie murmured.

He could feel tiny little shivers trembling through her body as he gently ran his thumbs across the fabric covering her nipples. "Baby, I want to take your gown down a little. Okay, baby?"

Her eyes were smoky with desire as she nodded her head. Jackie was conscious of the slow downward travel of his eyes as he took his time lowering her gown. He helped her to free her arms. The material stayed at her waist caught by the tie of her belt.

He groaned. He promised to be gentle, not to take any more than she wanted to give, to stop at any moment she wanted him to stop.

"Be my lover, Mitch Corey. Be my lover," Jackie whispered.

"Jackie," Mitch breathed. His hands glided over her bare shoulders and then down to cup her breasts. He bent his head.

She felt the searing warmth of his mouth and his tongue, stroking each taut tip, sending an electric response radiating through her entire body. Her breathing became sporadic as his breathing became rushed. Jackie's pulse raced wildly.

Mitch untied the belt at her waist and then straightened up to watch her gown fall revealing the bikini panties that she wore. He ran a finger sensitively across the silk and lace wanting to take them off, but he waited. Her eyelids lowered. He lovingly kissed her mouth.

Jackie moved to him and slid his shirt down his arms. With a low groan, he pressed her close. The bulge of his jeans established a place for itself. The coarseness of the denim teased her femininity even through her panties. A rushed moan escaped Jackie's parted lips to be captured by Mitch's mouth.

Her hands roamed over his back, feeling the movement of muscles beneath her touch. She parted her legs slightly. Her hips swayed against his, unconsciously encouraging the friction of his jeans. Her body throbbed with a need that she'd never felt before.

She placed kisses along his neck and his shoulders. She moved her hands down his chest. Her fingers trailed the band of his jeans. She reached to touch him more intimately, but hesitated. He raised her hand and pressed a kiss on her opened palm. Then he placed her hand over the denim where his arousal pushed hard. His body shook. Thrillingly, Jackie kissed his mouth. Her hand timorously caressing him.

His mouth left hers to feed on the softness of her breasts again and then to cross her belly. Very slowly, taking care to sense even the smallest resistance from her, he peeled her panties down. He made a guttural sound deep in the back of his throat as she allowed him to help her step free. He gently parted her thighs as his hungry mouth sought out her sweetness.

She chose then to stop him.

"Don't. Please," Jackie cried, pressing her thighs together, shocked by what he'd been about to do.

Mitch raised himself to her. She was trembling badly. He was trembling as well. With one arm around her waist, he held her as he brushed a wisp of damp hair off her forehead. "It's okay, baby," Mitch whispered, holding her possessively. With a slight bend of his knees, he swung her up in his arms and then he laid her down on the grass.

Crouching, his eyes moved over the pure perfection of her. "I want to kiss you everywhere," Mitch murmured fervently as he slid a hand between her thighs. "I want to . . ." He couldn't find more words to make her understand his burning need to know every inch of her.

His words set her body on fire, leaving her weak and pliant and wanting whatever he wanted. At his coaxing, Jackie opened her legs to him and felt his ragged breathing shiver across her stomach.

He kissed the center of her femininity. She arched frantically and then she was squirming away from him, trying to fight off what he knew was happening to her. Intuitively, he understood that the feeling of losing herself frightened her.

"Baby, it's okay," Mitch soothed. "I just want to please you."

Her eyes opened and then her lashes lowered as his face came close to hers. She kissed him hotly.

110

"Will you let me come inside you?" Mitch asked. In answer, Jackie struggled to find the zipper of his jeans but she couldn't manage to. Mitch stood up and got undressed.

Arms straight and rigid, he lowered himself over her. "Let it happen with me," he murmured, barely breathing as she wrapped her legs around him. He held one hand beneath her bottom, pushing her up to him as he entered.

Mitch kept his rhythm slow and easy. Little by little, Jackie moved with him as her excitement built with the pressure of each of his thrusts. She felt the sensations combining into one growing whorl of passion, the force of which stunned her. Her nails dug urgently into his shoulders. Jackie grinded her hips up to him.

In response, he went a little wild with her, but it was all right. She went a little wild with him. He plunged deeper and harder as she willingly surrendered to him. He took her mouth, claiming her lips as he claimed her entire body, giving entirely of himself.

Nothing else existed for Jackie but the feel of Mitch, the taste of Mitch, the smell of Mitch, the fire that was Mitch . . . She gave herself to him, abandoned herself, her memory, her past and her present. When it came, at the instant he erupted inside of her, she closed her eyes and she gave him her first climax too.

When she finally opened her eyes, she was sprawled on top of him. He had taken her with him when he'd rolled over. She smiled at him as her breathing returned to normal.

"How do you feel?" Mitch asked tenderly.

"Not bad," Jackie answered capriciously. Then she gave him a very sultry kiss.

He waited for her to finish kissing him and then he whacked her bottom playfully. "Not bad! Are you teasing me?" He stroked the same spot he'd just smacked.

"Yes," Jackie whispered, snuggling into him. "I feel unbelievably wonderful."

For long minutes, he ran his fingers through her hair, combing out some grass, and then he moved his hands languidly all over her.

"I like this," Jackie murmured.

"What do you like?"

"The way you're touching me now even after the passion."

Mitch smiled against her hair and decided not to tell her that he was on his way to becoming fully aroused again.

"We should get back to the castle," Jackie whispered while Mitch drew lazy circles on her back with his thumbs.

"Don't you ever tell me again that you're not passionate. Do you understand?"

"Yes." Jackie smiled, twisting a little against him, her body enjoying the rougher texture of his.

"I have half a mind to strangle that ex-husband of yours," Mitch said emotionally. How could the guy not have had enough brains to appreciate her?

Jackie slid up a little to kiss his mouth.

"Did you love him very much?" He sensed that there was still some hurt left in her and he wanted to assuage it with words.

Jackie stiffened slightly. He was choosing a subject

112

that she didn't want to discuss, yet she did want him to know everything there was to know about her.

"I told myself that I loved him," she answered. "I wanted to be in love with him. But I guess you can't make yourself love someone."

"I don't understand," Mitch said. "Weren't you in love with him when you married him?"

"I don't think so . . . No, I wasn't in love with him." She felt his hands just resting loosely on her now, not moving.

"If you weren't in love with him, then why did you marry him?"

"I'm not sure that I can make you understand." She eased herself off of him and then sat down at his side, crossing her legs under her.

Mitch locked his fingers behind his neck to prop his head. "Try me."

"I was young. I didn't care what I had to do to make things happen for me. I wanted financial security and I thought the only way I could get that was through a man."

His eyes narrowed on her. "I thought you told me that he was a struggling actor."

"Yes, but he's also independently wealthy. He wasn't struggling in the financial sense." She studied his expression, knowing he was passing judgment on her.

"Are you really that money hungry?" he asked harshly. But then he knew the answer. Hadn't she already said that money was her true passion?

"I don't like the way you said that."

"Is there another way of putting it?"

She looked away from him.

113

"Didn't your mother ever tell you that money makes a cold lover?"

Pride brought Jackie to her feet. "My mother was too busy trying to collect child support for three kids. I guess she just didn't have time for much talking. Of course, I could have gone to my father for advice. But he was too busy trading Cadillacs every year and spending his weekly paycheck chasing after every woman in town. A man after your own heart, I'm sure."

Jackie put on her panties and then her gown. She'd wanted him to understand. There was more she could have told him but now her stubborn heart refused.

Mitch rolled to his feet and put on his shorts. He zippered himself into his jeans, watching her hunt for her sandals. She found them and tied them on. She started to walk off. He gripped her arm, impeding her progress.

Jackie pulled her arm away from him.

"Why the hell can't I understand you?" Mitch called out to her as she started off again. "Who are you, Jacqueline Lacey?"

Jackie stopped and turned back to him. "An enchantress," she said coldly, then she walked away quickly, letting the tears come.

He watched her climb up on her stallion. She sat astride with her gown hiked up to her thighs. Without once glancing his way, she kicked her long legs into the stallion's flanks. The horse shot forward and she rode with her face buried in its flying mane and her hair blowing in the wind.

All his suspicion about her returned on the cold wind of reason and worked its cynical impact. Maybe

114

he wanted it to. Maybe there wasn't any other way to break the spell of the golden-haired enchantress. Had he just fallen in love with a woman that he didn't know at all? Was the loving sweetness of her just an illusion?

CHAPTER SEVEN

Mitch rode on horseback out to the tournament field. Paul was waiting for him. It was late afternoon and he was the last of the men to receive instruction on the art of jousting. Jackie sat on the sidelines with the other ladies and the men who had already had a lesson from Paul. He'd had plenty of time to observe her ignoring him.

Paul stood holding two blunt-ended jousting sticks both of them cut much shorter than the ones that would have been used by true knights. Mitch slid off his horse and walked up to meet him.

"Are you ready to begin?" Paul asked.

"Anytime you are," Mitch answered.

"The idea is to learn how to knock me off my horse using the jousting pole," Paul began. They both wore full suits of armor. Paul's helmet was on the ground where he'd left it after finishing up with the last man. Mitch's helmet was propped against his hip where he held it with one hand.

"I watched long enough to get the idea," Mitch said indifferently. But he'd looked over at Jackie more times than he'd looked out at the field. Was she as mercenary as he'd thought when she'd first told him why she had gotten married? It had seemed the only conclusion to draw at the time. But where did that leave him? It left him set up for a well-deserved kick in the head. With all his smarts, he'd been jerk enough to fall for her.

"You've got this real bad attitude problem, man," Paul said indolently. He didn't know how far Jackie would let him go before she got furious but he would like nothing better than to give Mitch Corey a lesson he wouldn't forget.

"Sweet talking me isn't going to make it any different, man," Mitch countered. He felt all bottled up inside and, yes, if the truth be known he wouldn't have minded a fight. But the fight had nothing to do with Paul.

Jackie watched Mitch put on his helmet and then take the jousting stick Paul handed him. How could he have loved her so tenderly and then have judged her so uncaringly?

Nina blew a trumpet signaling the instruction was to begin.

Maggi poked Jackie lightly on her arm. "If I were enough years younger I'd give you a run."

Jackie looked at her blankly.

"Mitch Corey." Maggi smiled. "And I say it's high time that you let a man into your life."

"He's not in my life," Jackie said, withholding any show of emotion.

"You're talking to me now, Jacqueline. Don't tell me there is nothing going on. I've seen the way the two of you look at each other."

"Please, Maggi," Jackie said, her voice breaking.

117

"What's the matter, honey?" Maggi saw a glint of moisture in Jackie's eyes.

"Nothing is the matter." Jackie looked straight ahead, not seeing anything.

"You're in love with him, aren't you?" Maggi asked softly.

Jackie turned her head aside and a curtain of silk hid delicately pained features. She didn't answer.

Mitch blocked Paul's jousting stick with the shield in his left hand. He felt the jolt of Paul's challenge shoot painfully up his arm and into his shoulder. It was the second attempt Paul had made to unseat him. The first one had been more or less a tease. This one wasn't.

Mitch braced himself in the saddle and used the heels of his boots to spur his horse for a retaliating charge against Paul. He hit up against Paul's shield and felt the jarring impact in his own body.

Paul lifted up the visor on his helmet to taunt. "Is that the best you've got, Corey?"

"Just warming up," Mitch retorted.

Both men rode apart and then both men charged—poles tangled, bodies arched forward—both men retreated to begin again.

Mitch felt every muscle in his body taut and straining. There was a skill to what he was doing but it was not a skill that he had learned. But where the challenge should have become all-encompassing to him, it failed.

Showing off, Paul swung his body out to the side of his saddle as he delivered his pole in perfect aim against Mitch's shield.

Mitch turned his horse back, lifting his visor as he

118

did to get some air on his face. He took a deep breath and turned to charge at Paul again, but Paul had taken time out to canter his horse before the spectators sitting on deeply cushioned lounge chairs.

Mitch rode up closer to Jackie.

Jackie could feel his gaze. She didn't look at him.

"You ready for some more?" Paul called out to Mitch.

Mitch dragged his eyes off Jackie and rode back out with Paul to the center of the field. Are you ready for some more, Corey? Are you ready to take a chance on being in love?

The first of the new blows Mitch fended nearly knocked him off his horse. Only sheer obstinacy kept his thighs tight enough to hold on.

Jackie blinked her eyes, not certain that she was seeing what she thought she was seeing. But she had been right. Paul wasn't giving Mitch instruction. The two of them were in full battle with each other. Her pulse jumped in alarm.

Paul tried to wave Mitch back with his jousting pole just as Mitch started to charge. Paul had spotted Jackie running out on the field. It took Mitch a half second longer to see her. He pulled in on the reins so sharply that he nearly unseated himself when his horse reared up on its hind legs.

Mitch took off his helmet and then climbed down from his horse, as did Paul.

"Just what do the two of you think you're doing?" Jackie practically shrieked. Her eyes went to Mitch and then Paul and then back to Mitch again. Didn't he know that he could have been hurt? Or was hurt . . .

119

Heart racing, Jackie looked for any sign of distress on his face.

"I guess we both got a little carried away," Mitch said, his expression void and unreadable.

Jackie clenched her fists at her sides. "Carried away? I'm running a business. I can't afford to let you get carried away." She gave him one long look from sad eyes and then she turned and walked.

"I want to talk to you," Mitch said, walking after her.

"Well, I don't want to talk to you." Jackie's defensiveness was mixed with anger and hurt.

"You're acting ridiculous. We have to talk." Mitch wiped at his forehead with the back of his hand.

"About what?" Jackie managed a sardonic laugh. "You already got what you wanted," she said and then she mimicked him. "It's your body I'm after, Ms. Lacey."

How could she even think that? Didn't she know that he would turn himself inside out for her, was turning himself inside out? No. How could she know? He hadn't told her.

He stood there deciding what to say to her but she had already called out to Maggi and then raced to catch up.

With jerky steps made more cumbersome because of the suit of armor he wore, Mitch walked to the castle. He caught a fast glimpse of Jackie from the back as she went into the kitchen with Maggi. She had her shoulders squared and her head angled in that proud way of hers that said she was intent on making herself unapproachable. Mitch sighed deeply and then went up the stairs.

Shannon turned to the door as Mitch let himself into his chamber. "What are you doing here?" Mitch asked, his face registering some surprise.

"Straightening up," Shannon answered, closing Mitch's closet door with her foot as she stepped away from it.

Mitch tossed his helmet on the bed. "I thought Nina was taking care of my room."

"We traded wings." Shannon took a stack of towels that she'd left piled on a narrow wormwood table into the bathroom. "How did you like jousting?" she asked, coming back out.

"I don't think *like* is a word I'd care to use." Mitch groaned as he twisted sore muscles trying to unlatch his armor.

"Here, let me help," Shannon said, moving up to him.

Mitch held his hands straight out, giving Shannon access to the metal closures at his sides.

"I could pour hot water into the tub for you, if you like," Shannon offered as she freed Mitch of his armor.

"Thanks, but I think a hot shower will do me fine." Mitch sat down on the edge of his bed to work at his chausses covering his thighs and legs. "How come you're taking care of rooms so late?"

"Gosh! It is late," Shannon exclaimed, heading quickly for the door. "I still have to change for dinner."

After Shannon closed the door behind her, Mitch fell back on the bed with only one set of his chausses undone. "Are you in love with her?" he asked himself out loud. There was an edge in his voice that was a plea for denial. But no denial came. Now what? he asked himself. But who did he think he was kidding trying to reason any of it out? What other choice did he have than to save her from herself? He was in love with her and that superseded all of his priorities.

The feast on the first night of instruction was one of Clayton's most fanciful efforts. Jackie was in the kitchen helping Clayton with some last-minute touches. Tonight, Jackie welcomed the excuse not to spend too much time in the great hall.

Mitch looked for the enchantress the minute he walked in. It was Maggi who told him that Jackie was taking her place working with Clayton this evening.

"Do you think it would be all right if I go into the kitchen?" Mitch asked.

"Clayton will have a fit and if he gets rattled, he'll get Jackie even more upset. I assume it's Jackie that you want to get to." Maggi gave Mitch a knowing look.

"Yes," Mitch answered.

"Are you going to straighten things out with her?" Maggi sounded more than a little bit worried and completely protective.

Mitch heard both of the messages in Maggi's voice. "You're very close to her, aren't you?"

"I care about her as if she were my own daughter and she cares about me more than my natural daughter would," Maggi replied. "Jackie has this special loving in her that she gives to the people she takes into her heart."

"She doesn't let too many people in though, does she?" The inflection in Mitch's tone made the question more a statement.

122

"The girl grew up hurt and it made the woman cautious." Maggi smoothed the folds of her mauve-colored costume gown.

"Tell me . . ." Mitch started to ask Maggi more about Jackie but Josh, dressed again as Merlin, came up to interrupt.

"Ah, Queen Morgan le Fay," Merlin said, addressing Maggi. "How gracious of you to delight King Arthur's court with your presence."

"I wonder that my half-brother Arthur will think so," Maggi responded coyly, playing her role.

"It is not he who carries ill will," Merlin said. "But it is you that plots him poor favor and all because he affronted you by passing over your son, Sir Baudemagus and choosing Sir Tor to offer the last seat at the Round Table."

Mitch watched the playacting between Maggi and Josh, as did Shannon, who had appeared in her red gown. A couple of the other vacationers had moved nearer to listen.

"I can do very little to safeguard him, though you had chosen to teach me of your art when I was yet a young damsel," Morgan le Fay said to Merlin.

"So it must be," Merlin said. "But still my power of prophecy bids me be wary of you."

"What prophecy is that?" Mitch asked as the players paused.

"Well, Sir Lancelot," Merlin said, fingering his phony white beard. "It has been given to me the gift of foresight to see into the future and it is Queen Morgan le Fay who will send unto me Vivien and it is Vivien who will capture my heart and make me slave to her will. And in the end, if legend must continue, it is

Vivien who will cause me to be placed in a great coffer of stone from which I cannot escape. Is that not so, my beautiful Vivien?" Merlin took Shannon's hand to his lips and then, without saying more, he led her off to the dance floor.

Maggi watched Shannon and Josh dancing. "They dance very well together," she commented.

Mitch hadn't been noticing Shannon and Josh. He was watching the entry for Jackie. He looked over at the dancers now and saw a perfect blend of bodies as they made some fancy turns. "It looks like they've been practicing that for a while." Mitch rotated his shoulders. The long hot shower he had taken had not alleviated much of the soreness in his muscles.

"I guess they must have gone to the same dancing school because they just met for the first time on this tour," Maggi said, her eyes still on the couple.

Mitch had already shifted the direction of his gaze. Jackie had walked into the hall carrying a silver tray of sweet rolls. Mitch left Maggi and started toward Jackie. She wore a simpler gown than the one she'd worn last night. This one was a pale blue and flowed more subtly. A narrow scarf encrusted with opal beads was tied around her forehead, making a headband that tamed her long hair. Even though she wasn't playing her role this evening, she still caused a stir in the room and she still turned male heads.

"Let me take that for you," Mitch said, putting his hands on the tray, but she wouldn't let go. He sensed her sharp intake of breath as her eyes met his.

"Will you please go back to enjoying the fantasy and leave me alone," Jackie said, giving him a hard, even look that effectively held back her tears.

"You are my fantasy," Mitch said quietly while she pulled the tray so tightly to her waist he thought she was causing herself pain.

Jackie turned on her heels, leaving Mitch staring after her. She felt another threat of tears. She squeezed her eyes shut and then opened them, barring the mist.

When she swung around after laying down the tray on the Round Table, Mitch was in front of her, blocking her way. "I want to talk to you alone," he said seriously.

"I don't want to talk to you," Jackie returned. Her head set proud, she skirted around him and walked purposefully to the exit of the great hall, heading back to the kitchen.

"How are you feeling, Lancelot?" Paul asked, approaching Mitch.

"Just fine," Mitch replied, feeling every ache singularly. But they didn't count. The only thing that counted to Mitch was getting back Jackie's heart and making everything right in the world for her. "What about you?" Mitch asked, after a pause in which a streak of masculine pride asserted itself.

"A little exercise like you and I had makes me feel invigorated." Paul felt more than a few aches and pains himself.

"King Arthur," Maggi said, coming up to speak to Paul. "Merlin asks that you join him for a moment."

Mitch looked off to see Josh in the middle of four of the vacationers. The tall leggy brunette was among them.

Once Paul had taken off to join Josh, Mitch tried to twist some of the stiffness out of his upper arms.

"You had some workout today," Maggi said, noticing.

"You can say that again." Mitch kept his eyes on the entry.

"She won't be coming out of the kitchen until after we've feasted," was what Maggi said.

Mitch brought his gaze to Maggi. "What time will she be finished cleaning up?"

"She should finish up with Clayton by about one o'clock providing he doesn't have any tantrums."

"Why does she put up with him?"

Maggi smiled fully. "She puts up with him because he is one of the people she cares about. Now, Sir Lancelot, are you ready to feast?"

Mitch gave Maggi a faint smile. "If you'll excuse me, Queen Morgan, I'm not in the mood for a party tonight."

Maggi nodded understandingly and then, after Mitch left the great hall, Maggi marched straight to the kitchen.

"What are you doing in here?" Jackie asked, startled at seeing Maggi walk in.

"I thought you should know that Mitch went up to his chamber," Maggi answered. "He didn't look right. I think he may have pulled some muscles, or worse, from his exhibition with Paul."

That report was sufficient to send Jackie's pulse beating double time in panic. "Do you think he needs a doctor?"

"I don't know, honey, but I think you should look in on him," Maggi said guilelessly.

"I'll send Josh," Jackie answered quickly. She couldn't handle being alone with Mitch.

Maggi took hold of Jackie's arm. "Josh is busy being Merlin. Jacqueline, go and see him yourself."

Clayton inserted a complaint. "I'm not taking care of the rest of the feast alone."

"I'm switching back with Jackie," Maggi said, grabbing a long apron from a hook.

Jackie was indecisive for a second, thinking she should just insist that Maggi go and see if he needed a doctor.

"Go," Maggi said, giving Jackie a small push.

Mitch got out of his knight's costume and put on a pair of beige slacks and a short-sleeved tan pullover. He sat down on the bed and snapped open his saxophone case.

Jackie stayed outside of Mitch's chamber door for a long while working on her composure. Hugging one arm to her waist, she finally knocked.

"Come in," Mitch called out, resting the mouthpiece of his horn against his mouth.

Jackie stepped in.

He didn't know who to expect but he hadn't expected her. His heart kicked into a fast tempo.

Swallowing, Jackie couldn't say anything right off. "Maggi thought you might be hurt from your jousting with Paul. I just came to check." She rushed her words when she did get them out.

"I'm fine." Mitch laid his saxophone down and then pitched his feet off the side of the bed but he remained sitting. What if she shut him out when he told her the truth about himself? He'd knew he had to tell her tonight.

"Well . . ." Jackie said skittishly. "I just wanted to check. If you think you need one I can send Josh to St.

Mary's for a doctor." She put a hand out behind her back to reach for the door handle.

"Jackie," Mitch whispered, his voice thick with emotion.

Jackie's hand flew off the door handle as if the metal had just turned red hot. Her green eyes fixed hypnotically on Mitch as he got to his feet and stayed on him as he walked to her.

Mitch reached out to touch her hair. Jackie swerved around, not to face him. She knew there were tears in her eyes.

"What do you want from me?" Jackie asked shakily.

Mitch ran his arm around the front of her waist, drawing her back against him. He felt the involuntary quiver in her body as he cushioned her to him.

When he didn't say anything, she spoke again. "You only get to make one conquest in this fantasy," she said, finding she couldn't say it with the anger she wanted to show him.

"Look at me," Mitch pleaded. "Come on, Jackie. Look at me." His hands urged her to turn in his arms and when she did, his hands still held her close to him.

"You're wrong in what you are thinking," Mitch said insistently. "You are not a conquest to me or a fantasy. I made love to you. Love, Jackie. I'm in love with you."

"No," Jackie said, shaking her head, not believing, afraid to believe.

"Yes," Mitch said, feeling her tremble. "And you're in love with me. You told me and you showed me that you are."

Jackie looked at him with eyes that begged for more assurance.

"I love you, Jackie . . ." Mitch untied the scarf at her temple, tossing it to the floor. "I love you, baby." He slanted his head, moving closer to her mouth. And then he kissed her and her arms came up to cling tenaciously to his neck.

"I-I want to tell you things," Jackie said haltingly when he took his mouth off hers.

Mitch kept her tight to him. "We'll talk," he said in a raw voice. "But later. Okay, baby?" He tried to mentally prepare himself for later because he would tell her everything then; who he really was and what he'd come seeking. But he couldn't prepare for that.

There were tears streaming down her face, happy tears. "Okay." Jackie's voice broke.

Mitch wiped at her tears and then rocked her in his arms.

"I love you, Mitch," Jackie said softly as she tipped her head back to look up at him.

"Again." His command was obvious.

"I love you," Jackie answered obediently. "I love you, I love you, I love you." She reached for his hands still around her while she gave him a smile that he didn't understand.

"What?" Mitch asked as she tried to disentangle his arms.

"I want you," Jackie said brazenly. "I want you over on that bed." Her cheeks became flushed. Being this kind of brazen was a first for Jackie.

When Mitch just stood unmoving with his blue eyes glistening at her, Jackie shyly asked, "You do want me now, don't you?"

"Do I want you now?" Mitch nuzzled the curve of her neck, holding her hair in one hand while he let her lead him with his other hand to the bed. "I want you under me and wrapped around me permanently," Mitch said, sitting down on the bed and pulling Jackie onto his lap. "I want to kiss you, touch you, love you. Always."

Jackie tugged his shirt out from the back of his slacks and began to remove it. "I need you so badly, Mitch. I do," she said, her eyes desirous. All of her restraints, her inhibitions, and her defenses were gone.

Mitch placed a whisper of a kiss on her lips and then he raised his hands for her to pull off his shirt.

Jackie caught Mitch flinch as she yanked his shirt off. "You are hurt," she accused.

Mitch took his shirt from her hand and threw it aside. "Will you make it better?" he whispered huskily, lifting her up on his lap to nip gently at her nipples through the fabric of her gown and her bra.

"Yes." Her one word was a breathy moan.

"I love you, Jackie." He kissed her feverishly with one hand holding the back of her neck while his other hand rode up her legs, sending pale blue silk into waves.

"Mitch . . ." Jackie moaned again as his fingers slid intimately to her lace panties.

"Tell me again," Mitch ordered, stilling the fingers that were pleasurably bothering her.

"I love you, Mitch," Jackie said. "I want to make love to you the way you've made love to me. Tell me how to thrill you. Show me . . . I haven't learned how to make love to a man."

Mitch groaned, emitting the breath she'd just

robbed him of as she eased off his lap. "I don't know how much of you I can handle." He smiled up at her sexily.

"I don't think you have to worry," Jackie said timorously, baring her shoulders as she drew down her gown. "I probably won't be that good."

Mitch yanked her back down to his lap. Her gown bunched around her feet. "You are an enchantress—the ultimate enchantress." He cradled her face between his hands, forcing her to give him her full attention. "And you have enchanted me. No one but you could do that. Do you understand what I'm telling you?"

Her green eyes held his blue ones and what his eyes were telling her was all she cared to know. He loved her.

He took her bra off. She felt it tighten first as he worked at the hooks, then loosen before coming off in his hands. He sent it sailing across the room.

Jackie stopped him as he started to taste her breasts. "You make me mindless when you do that."

"I like you mindless." He rolled his tongue over one already hard rose-tipped peak.

Jackie kicked her gown free of her legs and then she arched back away from him, holding on to his shoulders as she did.

"I want to undress you," Jackie said in a throaty voice.

Mitch brought his hand to the back of her neck and brought her mouth to his for a wild clashing of tongues and ardor. "You are setting me on fire, my enchantress," he growled at her.

131

"I like you on fire," Jackie teased, scooting off his lap and then insistently prodding him to stand.

"Can I take these off first?" He toyed with the elastic of her powder-blue bikini panties.

Jackie opened the buckle of his belt. "No." She sent her hair flying when she shook her head.

"Have I told you that you are absolutely and incredibly beautiful?" His hands came around her waist, hampering her as she tried to get his zipper down.

"Yes." Jackie smiled, sliding her hand between their two bodies so that she could finish.

"Jackie." At the same time that he said her name, he lifted her up off her feet and then let her slip down his body while he held her securely. "Baby, don't do anything that doesn't feel right for you. Don't try to please me unless you are pleasing yourself. Promise?"

Jackie looked into his eyes, all serious now. "I promise," she whispered against his mouth and then she kissed him. She kissed his lips. She kissed his shoulders. She planted kisses across his bare chest. She took down his slacks, helping him to step free of them. Then she hesitated with her hand over his jockey shorts, close to touching his arousal.

Mitch groaned and then he clasped the hand of hers that was threatening to drive him crazy. He didn't place it where she wanted it to be and where he wanted it to be. Instead, he swung her up in his arms and carried her over to the bed. "Baby, I need to be one with you," Mitch said urgently, taking off her panties and then ridding himself of his shorts.

But Mitch didn't bring his body over hers until he'd made sure that she was ready. Jackie was deliriously mindless by the time Mitch was certain. He entered her and she moaned and cried to him with her need as she welcomed his thrusts. He shuddered, holding himself back, waiting to be sure that she was with him. When the movement of her hips told him that she was, he let all his love and passion erupt, feeling complete emotional and physical satisfaction. And in that second of perfection, there were two hearts that beat as one.

Turning her over on top of him, Mitch crushed Jackie so tightly that she complained. "You're not letting me catch my breath." She giggled a little when he loosened his hold.

Keeping an arm slung around her waist, he raised himself up against the headboard with her back to his chest. Jackie rested her head on his shoulder, her hair tickling his neck. Mitch pressed his mouth to her temple, still damp from passion. "There are things that I have to tell you," he said slowly.

Jackie heard despondency in his voice. She shivered. "What things?" Her heart cried out to him. *Please don't say anything that will end what we've been sharing.*

"Jackie, I love you." His arm tightened around her. "Please, baby, promise that you'll love me no matter what."

She shivered more. "I promise."

Mitch pulled the quilt up from the other side of the bed and covered the two of them. "Jackie, I'm going to say this all the way through. Don't say anything until I've finished. Okay?"

"Okay," Jackie said quietly.

"I don't own a nightclub." Mitch started off in a troubled voice. "I don't make my living playing a saxophone. I'm a private investigator. I didn't come on this tour because I wanted a vacation. I came to—" He paused to take in a hard breath.

"To investigate someone?" Her voice was filled with surprise and confusion.

"Yes." Mitch sighed.

Jackie felt a tremor travel through his body. "Who are you investigating?"

"You—I came to investigate you."

"Me? Why would you be investigating me?"

"Baby, I want to help you. I will help you. I'll never let anything happen to you. Will you trust me?" Mitch begged.

"Trust you about what?" Jackie struggled against him because she wanted to turn and look at his face. He kept her from moving.

"Jackie, are you fencing jewelry through these tours?"

"Fencing jewelry? What are you talking about?"

This time when she pushed to turn to him, he let her. She looked into his face and he looked into hers. "Jackie, I will protect you but you have to be honest with me."

"I honestly don't know what you're talking about."

"Don't you, Jackie?"

"No, I don't, but I wish you would explain it to me. What do you mean by fencing jewelry? What jewelry?"

"Jackie, I have good reason to believe that this operation of yours is a front for taking stolen jewelry from LA and selling it out of the country."

"That is absolutely absurd! What reason do you have for thinking that?"

"The reason doesn't matter. Only the answer matters. Are you involved in anything illegal, Jackie? You can tell me, baby, because I promise you that I will help you."

Jackie touched his face, half-smiling, her lip trembling. "I'm not. Honestly, I'm not. You have to believe me. Mitch . . . ?"

"God, baby, I love you." Mitch groaned, wanting to believe her and believing her because he wanted to.

"Me too." Jackie offered him the most beautiful smile that he'd ever seen on her face. "I love knowing that you would champion me if I needed you to. You are truly my knight."

Mitch kissed her mouth and that smile until he had to break for them to both gasp for air. "I was tearing myself up worrying about you being involved with fencing jewelry."

"I wish you had just asked me sooner," Jackie said breathlessly with his kiss still on her lips. "I'll always tell you anything you want to know."

Mitch cocked an eyebrow at her and then he took both her hands and pinned them over her head, pressing them to the pillow. "There is something else I want to know. What the hell have you got going with Vic Logan?"

Jackie's eyes widened in surprise. "Vic Logan is Gregg Allen's father and my father-in-law . . . Or he was my father-in-law. I still love him as my father-in-law. How did you even know to ask?"

"Girl." Mitch grinned. "You have not been out of my sight for long since the first day I met you."

"Really?" Jackie asked, laughing as he playfully manhandled her.

"I don't intend to ever let you out of my sight for long." Mitch let her hands down and she immediately wrapped them around his neck. "Do you have any idea how good I feel right now?"

"How good do you feel right now?"

"I feel like I just reached the end of the rainbow."

Jackie grinned. "What's it like at the end of the rainbow?"

"Kiss me, gorgeous, and I'll show you."

CHAPTER EIGHT

"You don't really want me to go, do you?" Mitch groaned, snuggling the back of Jackie's warm body against the front of his.

Jackie turned in his arms so that she faced him. She kissed his closed eyes. "You were supposed to leave my bed no later than three A.M. and it is close to seven A.M. now." Her sleepy voice held no censure. She hadn't really wanted him to leave.

"Do you really think that you are fooling anyone by sending me padding back to my own chamber before they all wake up?"

Jackie pressed her face to Mitch's chest. Her hair fanned out in tangled disorder across his shoulder. "Two more nights and you'll be padding back to your own apartment," she said, muffling her voice intentionally, not wanting him to hear any of the desperation she had been feeling for the past day and a good part of the night. They would be back in LA soon and she couldn't stop herself from worrying about how that would affect their relationship.

"I've been thinking about that," Mitch said.

"What have you been thinking?" Jackie tilted her head back against the pillow to look at him. The sun hadn't yet brightened the room. In the fading light of the tapers, she could just barely make out his expression. She kept her features unrevealing.

"I've been thinking that we have to come to some decision. Are you going to live with me or am I going to live with you?" Under the covers his hands touched and teased.

"You mean that you want us to live together?" Jackie felt her mouth go dry. She had thought about it and not quite rejected the idea. But now that he'd said it, she knew it really wasn't what she wanted.

His hands cradled her breasts. "I want to be with you every moment that I can. Don't you want that too?" He asked himself if he was offering her enough. Did she want marriage? Did he?

"I suppose we can try it out for a while. You can stay with me for a few days and then I'll stay with you. Maybe we should see how it is living together before either of us hands in our keys." Guardedly, Jackie kept her voice light, joking to break the mood, afraid to deal with him seriously. Did she want him to ask her to marry him? She'd been telling herself no. She didn't want to chance marriage. She didn't want another marriage like the one she'd had. Nor did she want a marriage like the one her parents had. If there was one thing she'd learned, it was never to trust love to be permanent.

"I have to get dressed," she said, sitting up. "I'm going with Clayton to St. Mary's to pick up what we need in food supplies to finish up the fantasy."

Mitch tumbled Jackie back down over him. "You didn't answer. Don't you want us to live together?" he asked.

138

"Can we finish discussing this later? I do have to get dressed." She tried to pry his hands off from around her. "You have to get dressed yourself. Paul will be getting all the men together soon for the hunt. How are you doing with the bow and arrow anyway?" She rambled nervously while he looked into her eyes.

"Marry me," Mitch said as she wound down.

Jackie pushed angrily at him to release her.

"What's the matter?" He tried to hold her still. "Don't you want to marry me?"

Jackie glared down at him. "I'm not holding out for marriage. You make me feel as if I'm trying to coerce you into asking," she said tensely.

"Oh, Jackie," Mitch whispered miserably. "I know that you aren't trying to coerce me. I did ask you impulsively. I hadn't thought about it ahead of time or even thought about ever getting married again. But I am thinking now. I love you, Jacqueline Lacey. Will you marry me?"

"I don't think you should be asking me . . ." Jackie buried her face in the pillow behind Mitch's head.

"Why? What is it, Jackie? Baby, what's wrong?"

"Nothing . . . just nothing."

He stroked her with his hands. "Don't shut me out. Tell me what you are thinking. Do you love me?"

"I do love you," Jackie said, lifting her head. "I just don't want you to ask me to marry you . . . Not now."

"Did you fall in love with a saxophone player and not a private investigator?" He released a ragged breath. "Is that it?"

"No, that's not it. But I did hate you lying to me. I

139

was very upset that you did." But she had been more than just upset. When she'd thought about it afterward, it terrified her how convincingly he had lied.

"And now? Are you still upset?"

"No." She did rationally understand his motives but emotionally she was confused.

"Are you afraid of marriage?"

"Yes, I'm afraid. If I get married again I want to be sure that it's forever. I want to be sure of that feeling."

"What aren't you sure about—what you feel or what I feel?"

Jackie turned onto her back. "I'm sure that I love you. But I need some time. Mitch, I don't think that I can handle another marriage that fails."

Mitch folded his pillow in half. His head raised, he turned toward her. "Tell me about Gregg Allen?"

"What do you want to know?"

"Everything. How old were you when you met him?" Mitch asked, prompting her to start.

"The first time I met him I was going on nineteen. His father—that's Vic Logan—introduced us. I was training then to become a stunt woman and working on the same lot where Vic was directing a movie."

"A stunt woman?" Mitch interrupted, smiling in surprise.

"Yes." Jackie smiled back.

"I can't picture you as a stunt woman."

"That's because you don't know that there is a part of me that likes risk taking. I did enjoy the idea of getting close to danger, knowing I could control the circumstances."

"Do you know how very much alike we are? That's

exactly the way I felt when I first became a police-man."

"A policeman?"

"Before I went out on my own," Mitch explained. "So what happened to your career as a stunt woman?"

"I was never quite able to master the technique." Jackie looked at him with an impish grin. They both laughed and then they both became serious again.

"Vic was going to use me in the movie he was doing at the time," Jackie said. "But when it came to shoot-ing, I fluffed the stunt and he had to use someone else. Vic felt so bad about having to replace me that he took me for lunch that day to the commissary. We ran into Gregg there and the three of us ate together. Actually, we all ate very little. I was depressed at not having been able to do the stunt and Vic and Gregg spent the hour arguing."

"What did they argue about?" Mitch asked.

"Gregg wanted Vic to give him a starring role in one of his movies and Vic insisted that Gregg first make it on his own. It was an ongoing argument and is still going on now."

"Do you still see Gregg?"

"No," Jackie answered. "Just Vic."

"I assume Gregg asked you out that first time you met."

"Yes, but I said no. I didn't see Gregg again until a year later when I had gotten a job with a casting agency. I didn't know it at the time, but Vic had set that job up for me. I thought I had gotten it on my own."

"I don't know that I'm thrilled about Vic Logan's interest. Are you sure he hasn't got designs on you?"

"I'm sure. He's been like a father to me."

"What about your father? Where is he?"

"He's living in New York. I don't hear from him, except for an occasional card at Christmas."

"What about your mother?"

"She had a heart attack and died when I was eighteen."

Mitch slipped his arm under Jackie, hugging her to him.

Jackie accepted his comforting for a moment and then she eased away. "Do you still think less of me because one of the reasons I married Gregg was for financial security?"

"No, baby," Mitch said. "I understand what it's like to want what money can buy and I understand it even more because I know you grew up without having much of anything."

"I didn't lie to Gregg," Jackie said quietly. "I told him that I didn't think that I loved him but that I wanted the kind of life-style he was offering me and that I also wanted to please Vic. Vic wanted me to marry Gregg."

"If Gregg knew that you didn't love him, why did he want to marry you?"

"Gregg wanted to please his father and he thought that after we were married, Vic would give him a good role in one of his movies. Only he didn't tell me that. He told me that he loved me and that in time I would love him. I wanted to make the marriage work. I wanted to love him. But we just didn't have those feelings."

"Are you sure that he didn't really love you?"

"Yes, I'm sure. He wanted me. I didn't understand

then that there is a difference between a man wanting a woman and a man loving a woman."

He heard the pain in her voice and he pieced together even more than she was saying. His jaw was set and his features rigid. "Were you a virgin when you married Gregg?"

"Yes." Jackie trembled, remembering how uncaringly Gregg had taken her that first time and the rest of the times in the two years she'd been married to him.

"Oh, baby. Come here and let me hold you." Mitch coaxed her back into his arms. When she came, he caressed her over and over again.

Jackie didn't want to cry but she couldn't seem to stop herself. "I-I was trying s-so h-hard to make it w-work. But h-he didn't c-care. He flaunted his a-affairs with other women. I-I had t-to and I-I took . . ." She didn't finish.

"What?" Mitch prompted her gently. "What did you have to do? What did you take?"

"I-I took . . ." Jackie began again through tearful fragments.

"What did you take?" He comforted her with feathery light touches. He silently promised to make sure she was never hurt ever again.

Jackie sat up abruptly. She squeezed her eyes shut hard and took deep breaths through her mouth. Mitch got out of the bed and went into the bathroom to get her some tissues. Sitting back down on the bed, he handed them to her.

Jackie blew her nose. "He said he was going to divorce me because marrying me had not gotten Vic to give him any part and because I-I wasn't good . . . in

143

bed." Jackie's eyes were lowered and her shoulders stooped.

"Baby, he didn't deserve anything from you. Do you understand what I'm saying?"

"Yes," Jackie answered, slowly meeting Mitch's eyes. "I don't feel that kind of hurt anymore. You took it away. But—but . . ."

"What?" He smiled at her and took hold of her hand.

Jackie bit down on her bottom lip. "Vic got very angry at Gregg when he found out we were getting divorced. He put the entire blame on Gregg. I didn't want there to be an even bigger rift between them, so I went to Vic and told him the real reason I had married Gregg. I . . ." Her eyes closed briefly and she paused.

Mitch put his arm around her. "What did you tell him?"

Jackie blew her nose again. "I told him that I was to blame. I should never have agreed to marry Gregg, not for the reasons that I did. I felt like I had cheated Vic and I wanted him to still love me. But I didn't think that he could and . . ."

"What did Vic say when you told him?" Mitch asked her gently.

Jackie threw her arms around Mitch's neck, wanting to be hugged and he hugged her. "I'm sure that Vic understood," Mitch said, speaking against Jackie's hair. "Didn't he, baby?"

Jackie nodded her head. "Do you call all women baby?" she asked suddenly, but it was something that had been on her mind.

Mitch took her face between his hands. "No, I don't call all women baby. I've never called any woman baby. I call you baby because sometimes, Jacqueline Lacey, I think of you as a little girl and that makes me feel very protective about you. I like the feeling." Mitch smiled. "Is that okay?"

"Yes," Jackie said, smiling tremulously. "But I am also very independent. I want you to know that. I have to be independent."

"I know." Mitch grinned and kissed her mouth lightly, tasting the salt of her tears. "What did Vic say when you told him?"

"He said a lot of things—things about Gregg not being mature and that he had hoped being married to me would make him more of a man. But that's not what I want to tell you. You see, Vic got me a lawyer —and I got a large settlement . . ."

"That's nothing to feel bad about. A judge made that decision and I bet he didn't even know the half of it." Mitch cuddled her to him.

"Mitch, I'm just not ready to place my trust in another marriage," Jackie whispered.

"I understand," Mitch murmured, knowing he was going to make sure that he proved to her that she could, no matter how long it took.

"I really should get dressed." She made no move to leave the security of his embrace.

"Do you feel better now?" His hands rode up under her hair and then down her back.

She felt his comfort change to sensuality even before he realized it. "I wish you could make love to me again right now," Jackie said in a wispy voice.

"I want to make love to you now." He raised her so that his mouth could easily enjoy one of her nipples.

"Clayton will be waiting," Jackie said. Then she moaned, forgetting about Clayton.

"He can wait," Mitch whispered, turning Jackie over his arm.

"But he'll come up here looking for me . . . He'll come." Giggling, Jackie squirmed away.

Mitch playfully caught her back up in his arms just as there was a knock on the door.

"Jacqueline, are you up yet?" Clayton Brooks called out impatiently.

"Yes," Jackie called back, making funny faces at Mitch that had him grinning and her laughing behind her hand.

"Tell him to wait for you downstairs," Mitch said, murmuring in Jackie's ear. Jackie opened her mouth to call out to Clayton. Mitch grabbed her back and kissed her thoroughly. Then he let her tell Clayton to go down and wait.

"We can't do anything now," Jackie said, her eyes teasingly admonishing him.

"I know," Mitch said, his blue eyes devilish. "But I want to touch you enough so that you can't think about anything else but getting back to me as soon as you can."

Jackie smiled. "I should be back in about three hours."

"Three hours . . ." Mitch groaned. Then he kissed her breasts, sliding his mouth from one to the other.

Jackie arched away from him. "If you keep doing that to me, I'm going to start doing things to you." She gave him a sultry smile, feeling so good with him. *Please,* she prayed. *Let it be real.*

146

"If you touch me . . ." Mitch grinned. "I'm not going to let you go until I've had my way with you."

Jackie scooted out of the bed and then she stood before him, a blush bringing high color to cheeks that had been pale not long ago. "Do you think it's all right for me to be as brazen with you as I've been getting?" she asked and then feeling silly and shy for having asked, she turned her back to him. "Forget that." She laughed, embarrassed.

Mitch said her name and she swung back around. "I think it's more than all right. I love you being brazen. Baby, you can be anything with me that you feel like being, except mad. You can't ever get mad at me."

"It's a deal."

Mitch smiled.

"I just realized," Jackie said as she got her underthings from a drawer in her bureau. "You're going to be on a hunt today with Paul and the other men. I'll be the one waiting for you to come back."

"I've decided to skip the hunt. I'm lousy with a bow and arrow and you know how I hate having Paul show me up," Mitch kidded.

"I'm going to start calling you baby for all your male childishness," Jackie kidded back as she stepped into the bathroom.

"Oh, baby, baby, what you do to me." Mitch sang until he heard Jackie turn the shower on. He wished Clayton weren't waiting for her.

When Jackie came back out in a pink bra and matching panties, Mitch was zippering himself into his jeans. He whistled at her. She pivoted around seductively for him. "Don't you have any pity on me?" Mitch groaned, only half-teasing.

"An enchantress never has any pity for a mere mortal man," Jackie said flirtatiously.

Mitch grinned. "Oh, sure, after the enchantress has taken herself a nice cold shower." He walked up, eyeing her warningly.

"Don't you dare." Jackie laughed, stepping back. "Go sit down on the bed and let me get dressed."

"I will if you say it first."

She knew what he wanted to hear. "I love you, Mitch Corey."

Mitch kissed her mouth and swatted her behind. Then he went over and sat down on the edge of the bed.

"Stay here for a while after I've left. I'll tell Paul that I saw you in the hall and that you won't be joining in the hunt." Jackie put on her jeans, a red polo shirt and her sandals. She felt uncomfortable about not acting strictly businesslike.

"How long do you want me to stay here?" Mitch indulged her. He doubted that there was a single person who didn't know that they were lovers.

Jackie glanced at her watch. "The women will all be joining Maggi, Nina, and Shannon for mud baths in a half hour. Wait until then."

"Okay." He watched her pick up her hairbrush. "Can I brush your hair for you?"

"No, you can just sit on that bed." She waved her brush threateningly at him before she pulled it through her hair.

His palms pressed to the mattress on either side of his thighs, Mitch watched her braid her beautiful long hair.

Finished, Jackie turned to him. "I like the idea that you wanted to brush my hair," she said happily.

"You'd better get out of here before I think up a few other things that I would like to do." He winked at her and she went, looking back at him once before she closed the door behind her.

Mitch picked up his gray jersey from the floor where he had dropped it last night. He started to pull it on and then changed his mind. He tossed it onto the bed, took off his jeans and his shorts and marched into Jackie's bathroom. He took a shower using her soap scented with heather and her shampoo that held the same fragrance. After that, he dried himself with a towel still damp from Jackie's body. Then he went downstairs and helped himself to coffee and sweet rolls from the buffet.

"I thought all the men went hunting with Paul," Josh said, looking startled as he walked into the small hall to find Mitch there drinking his coffee.

"I decided not to join them." Mitch noted that like himself Josh was dressed in jeans. "I guess Merlin doesn't join the hunt either."

"Merlin's face needs a rest from his whiskers. Besides, the only hunt Merlin might be interested in this morning would send him wading into mud," Josh joked as he helped himself to a cup of coffee.

"I thought Shannon Grant was giving the baths, not taking one," Mitch said knowingly.

"Who said anything about Shannon Grant? There are a couple of brunettes that I've had my eyes on."

Mitch would have sworn that whenever he had looked over at Josh in the last eight days, Josh's eyes had been on Shannon Grant.

149

"Of course, no one can miss noticing that you have eyes for only one particular lady," Josh commented, taking a danish from the buffet.

Mitch smiled. "Have you known Jackie for long?"

"I started out with her when she began the tours."

"That's right," Mitch said idly. "Jackie did mention that you, Clayton, Maggi, and Paul had been with her from the beginning." Jackie hadn't mentioned it. Mitch just knew that from when he'd been investigating Have a Fantasy Vacation as a possible fencing operation. He was overly relieved to have rejected that possibility.

"I guess then that she must have told you that I'm an actor."

"Yes, she did." He hadn't really had any conversation with Jackie about Josh. "Listen, let me know when you land a good role. I'll be sure to catch the movie."

"I've just about decided to throw the towel in."

"Does that mean that you'll be giving up these tours also?"

"I haven't decided about that yet. Do me a favor and don't mention anything to Jackie. I'll give her plenty of notice if I decide to quit."

"Okay." Mitch thought he might just go ahead and prepare Jackie.

"Well, I'm off." Josh put his cup down on the table. "I've got a magic show to rehearse for tonight."

Mitch drank another cup of coffee after Josh walked out. Then he left the hall, planning to go to his chamber. On his way there, he changed his mind and went back to Jackie's chamber. He knew the first thing she

150

would do when she returned would be to come up and change into a costume.

Mitch crossed to the bed and lay down to wait for her. He stayed prone for a little over an hour and then, feeling restless, he got up and walked around.

The pale pink sleeping gown she had worn when he had first come to her was on a woven rush chair where he had thrown it when he had taken it off her. Mitch folded it up and brought it over to her bureau. He smiled to himself as he came up with the thought of straightening up the room for her. Nina and Shannon took care of the other rooms, but Jackie took care of her own.

Mitch tucked the gown away. Then he made the bed but he turned the quilt down. The lilac silk gown she had on during last evening's festivities was draped over a light-green taffeta chaise longue. Mitch picked it up, along with two long strands of costume pearls that were lying under it. He hung the gown in her wardrobe and then he took the pearls over to a large wood-carved jewelry box that he had noticed on an end table. He raised the lid to lay the pearls in and then he froze.

He cursed out loud before his hands dropped the pearls and then sifted through, piece by piece, necklaces, rings, and bracelets—all of which had been stolen in LA during the last few months.

Mitch collapsed in the nearest chair. He bent his head and dropped his face to his hands. He sat that way for long minutes with a voice screaming frantically in his head. She wouldn't have lied. God, she couldn't have lied . . .

Could he have been taken in by a green gaze that

only pretended innocence? Had she really fallen in love with him as he had with her? Or had she only been playing a part?

He pictured her in his mind. He pictured those green eyes of hers saying that she loved him but the image blurred through a band of pain pressing at his temples. He breathed deeply, shoring up his strength, and then he stood. He left her chamber and went to his.

In the bathroom, he sloshed cold water on his face. Then he walked over to the wardrobe. He pulled out his saxophone case. He took his horn out, laying it on the floor. The felt bottom of the case lifted up easily. Mitch took out the insurance company's pictures that were concealed there, along with his license. It was as he was placing the bottom felt back in place that he realized that just now his license had been lying on top of the pictures. He knew, positively, that he had placed his license underneath the pictures. His heart pounded. A vein in his temple worked spasmodically. When had she found them? he asked himself. When? When had she discovered who he really was?

Jackie raced up the stone stairs after she'd helped Clayton store away his purchases in the ice room. She knew Mitch would be in her chamber, waiting. As she opened the door, her face glowed with excitement. They had never made love in the afternoon.

Mitch had his back to her, standing in front of the end table with the lid of her jewelry box opened. He was holding a 2½-karat diamond pendant that was hung on a gold chain.

Jackie called to him and Mitch turned around

slowly to face her. He casually twirled the chain around his finger while he studied her face.

"I couldn't wait to get back." She met his eyes and became confused by the hard look he returned.

"I'm flattered," he said coolly. "Or should I be? Maybe it wasn't me you were anxious to get back to."

"What's the matter?" she asked.

He stayed silent. His eyes remained on her.

"What's wrong?" She stumbled on.

"Nice piece, don't you think?" He held the pendant up.

She gave the necklace a cursory glance. Something pushed at her consciousness but didn't actually register.

"No comment?" he asked.

"Why are you acting this way?"

"Acting is more your game than mine."

"Mitch . . . What happened?"

"What happened, honey, is that I found these." Mitch dropped the pendant into the opened jewelry box. "Couldn't you have at least kept this stuff hidden? Oh, I forgot—you did say that you were getting brazen with me. Well, you didn't lie about that."

Jackie's hand was shaking as she took a topaz linked bracelet from the box. "This isn't . . ." She swallowed. "This isn't the jewelry that I brought with me. Is this the stolen jewelry you were talking about?"

"Is it? Baby, you know it is."

"I don't know anything about this jewelry. This is not the jewelry that I picked out at the studio. I haven't seen any of these pieces before. Anyway, none of this even looks real."

He almost laughed. "You may have fooled the customs inspectors by coating the stones but don't you remember, I have the pictures. Tell me, when did you find the pictures? When did you discover that I was a private investigator?"

"I don't know what you mean. You know when you told me."

"Right, I know when I told you," he said harshly. "But you knew before that, didn't you?"

"No," she denied.

He ignored her answer and continued. "I think you knew who I was before we made love that first time. I think you wanted me to fall in love with you. I think you were out to buy yourself some insurance. And it worked. You knew I would be sucker enough to protect you. But you had to lie to me because you're not in this alone and you couldn't be sure that I would protect whoever is in this with you. Who are you in this with? Is it Paul? Josh? Maggi? Clayton? Who?"

Surely he couldn't really think— "How can you believe what you are saying? I haven't lied to you. I'm telling you the truth. I don't know anything about this jewelry. This is the box I brought but these are not the pieces that I rented from the studio. Someone must have switched them."

"That's an interesting theory—one I even gave a thought to myself." His eyes mocked her. "Now who do you think it could be? Who else goes through customs with a box of jewelry besides you?"

She stood stiffly before him. "Well, Dick Tracy, you can just figure it out for yourself," she retorted defensively. She was doing some figuring out on her own. He had deliberately gone after her. He had wanted her to fall in love with him. But it had only been to get information.

He'd figured enough of it out already. He'd found his proof but he'd found it too late to keep from losing his heart. "I intend to find out who you're in this with." He picked up the box of jewelry. "I'll say this for you, Jackie. You sure know how to play the part of an enchantress. But then I don't suppose an enchantress needs a heart."

She watched him stride angrily to the door, then slam his way out taking the box of jewelry with him.

After he left, the enchantress crumbled down on her bed and cried her heart out.

CHAPTER NINE

"You look awful," Maggi remarked sympathetically after Jackie called out to her to come in.

"What time is it?" Groggy, Jackie dragged herself out from under the quilt to sit at the side of the bed. Pride had kept her up late last night. She hadn't left the festivities until after Mitch and he'd stayed until the last of the guests had retired. He hadn't spoken to her once during the evening. He'd hardly even acknowledged her presence.

"Nine o'clock," Maggi answered.

"Oh . . ." Jackie moaned. She bent her head down, making a curtain of honey-blond silk around her face while she tried to ease some of the tension in her shoulders and neck. She hadn't slept much at all. But her physical exhaustion wasn't even a close second to the emotional exhaustion she was feeling.

"Yes, oh . . ." Maggi corroborated. "You've got less than a half hour to get yourself dressed. Paul is waiting for you to start the tournament. Go take a fast shower, then I'll give you a little help from my makeup bag."

"Is Mitch downstairs?" Jackie asked, getting to her feet.

"Yes," Maggi responded. "I gather something happened between the two of you again."

"I don't want to discuss it," Jackie said quickly. "But I do want to know if he questioned you about anything either this morning or last night?"

"What do you mean— What would he question me about?" Maggi looked perplexed.

"Nothing . . . Never mind."

Maggi studied Jackie, who was looking all strained, her body taut with tension. "Don't you want to talk about it, honey?"

"No," Jackie replied shortly.

Maggi wanted to tell Jackie that it's bad to hold everything in, but she bit her tongue. Jackie walked toward the bathroom.

Maggi was dumping the contents of her cosmetic bag on the bed when Jackie came out of the bathroom in a terry robe after having taken a fast shower.

"This is not the start of a discussion," Maggi qualified as Jackie sat down on the bed with her. "But I think you should know that he looks like he's in even worse shape than you."

"I'm not interested." Jackie's voice came out sharp and pained.

"The subject is closed," Maggi assured her, offering a small smile. "Close your eyes, honey. Let me see what I can do to make you look like you haven't spent the night crying."

"I didn't spend the night crying," Jackie insisted. "I just didn't sleep well."

"Whatever you say," Maggi scoffed tenderly. She picked up a tube of cover-up from her pile of goodies.

"Maggi, how well have you gotten to know the group we have on the tour this time?"

"I haven't gotten to know this group any better than I've gotten to know any of the other groups." Maggi spread the cover cream underneath Jackie's eyes, erasing the dark shadows and concealing some of the puffiness. "Why do you ask?"

"I was wondering if you might have noticed anyone acting out of the ordinary?" Jackie opened her eyes as Maggi took her fingers away.

"What do you mean by out of the ordinary?" Maggi chose a wand of emerald green mascara and went back to work on Jackie's eyes.

"You know how everyone gets all involved in the fantasy after the first day or so of feeling shy." Jackie fought to keep her eyes from blinking. "Would you say that there was anyone in this group who seemed less involved?"

"I assume you mean other than you-know-who."

"Yes, other than Mitch."

"Well, let me see." Maggi stayed thoughtful for a moment. "There's Joan and Dave Kiernan. Those two should have just rented themselves a bed somewhere. They're making their own fantasy." Maggi grinned. "I think this is the first time we've had a honeymoon couple, isn't it?"

"Yes," Jackie answered, returning an appropriate smile. "Other than Joan and Dave . . . Is there anyone else?"

"Not that I noticed." Maggi opened a compact of blush and stroked color into Jackie's high cheekbones. "If you're worrying about everyone having a good time—don't. Everyone seems to be. Now what gown are you going to wear?" Maggi was dressed in a pearl-gray gown embroidered over with red threads and a cone-shaped hat covered with the same material. A long gossamer sheer white veil flowed from the point of her hat to billow behind her.

"I don't know," Jackie answered listlessly. "I haven't thought about it."

"Go put some gloss on your lips and brush your hair. I'll pick one out for you."

Jackie went over and looked at herself in her dressing table mirror. Maggi had done a perfectly wonderful job of erasing the ravage of tears, but the hurt in her green eyes went too deep to be disguised. How could she have been such an idiot? Even when she'd told herself to doubt Mitch Corey's feelings, in her heart she had begun to believe that the fantasy was real.

By the time Jackie and Maggi came out to the tournament field all the ladies, each dressed in colorful costumes, had taken their seats. Jackie wore an emerald green gown with a square neckline fashioned into a rolled collar that was overlaid with ecru lace. Her only adornment was a matching green headband studded with fake topaz gems.

Jackie looked out on the field as she took a seat next to Maggi. The archery targets had been lined up for the first of the contests. A red carpet runner was laid across the roughened dirt to serve as the mark from which each knight would demonstrate his skill. The knights, all in identically designed armor, waited in a long tent. To the side of the tent harlequin-robed horses, all similarly draped in the colors and emblems of King Arthur's court, stood ready.

159

Nina, in navy tights and a lighter blue puffed-sleeve overblouse that came down to her knees, sounded the trumpet and Merlin walked out from the tent and mounted one of the horses.

"Ah, fair damsels," Merlin called out, bowing in his saddle as he approached. "Before you will come the greatest knights of our land to do challenge and engage in battle. I do beseech of you some token for the knight to wear when that knight asks to do that lady honor as beckons the code of chivalry." Merlin rode back and forth in front of the ladies.

Once again, Nina heralded the trumpet. The knights, without helmets for this event, filed out of the tent to mount horses. The horses were all white stallions, the same as Merlin rode.

Paul cantered his stallion up to the ladies. Mitch guided his horse behind Paul as the other knights all fell in line.

Shannon called out to Mitch, waving a azure blue scarf that she had just untied from around her neck. "Sir Knight, I offer you a favor to take into the contest."

Jackie angled her head purposely to watch Mitch as he stopped his horse in front of Shannon. Jacqueline Lacey was not going to behave as if she couldn't handle herself.

There was an expressive pause while Mitch looked over at Jackie. His irises darkened as he was greeted by her air of aloofness.

"I am sorry, my lady," Mitch said, speaking politely to Shannon. "I cannot accept. There is another lady's favor that I seek."

Jackie felt a flutter of panic and her heart began to

160

beat wildly as Mitch cantered his horse the few paces it took to bring him directly to her.

"My Lady Nimue, will you honor me with your favor?" Mitch asked, loud enough to draw everyone's notice.

Jackie took in the effrontery of his arrogant pose: one shoulder insolently slumped toward her, the hand holding the reins resting comfortably on a maille-covered thigh. "Perhaps, Sir Knight, you would do best to choose another."

"I have chosen you and I have heard that in King Arthur's court no lady with a conscience would break a knight's heart by refusing to allow him to do her honor. Or doesn't the enchantress have a conscience?" Mitch asked calmly but he was tightly coiled. Despite the cards being all stacked up—despite the fact that she had taken him for a ride—despite it all, he was still in love with her.

Fighting hard to appear unruffled, Jackie slipped off her headband and handed it to him. With all eyes on her, she had no choice but to concede—that or let him continue to torment her.

"Will you put it on for me, my lady?" He eyed her coolly, challengingly.

Jackie had to stand on tiptoe even with him bending his insolent head. She kept her face averted from him. "Leave me alone," she whispered through a pasted-on smile.

"No way," Mitch taunted. Then he rode off, crossing the tournament field to tether his horse by the tent.

Jackie didn't pay any attention to who exchanged favors with whom, though she did notice that Paul had tied Shannon's blue scarf around his neck.

Maggi tapped her hand once but she didn't say a word. Jackie wouldn't have been able to answer if she had. She was concentrating all her efforts on not crying.

Paul rode out to the center of the field, stopping at the point from where he would judge the archery contest along with Josh.

Merlin proclaimed, "Let the tournament begin."

Wearing a sheath of arrows on their shoulders, the knights walked to the mark, each one holding a bow.

Shannon left her seat and came over to Jackie. "I hope I won't spoil anything," Shannon said, whispering. "I'm not feeling well. I'm going to lie down for a while. I must have eaten something that didn't agree with me last night."

Jackie nodded her head. Maggi said, "Stop by the kitchen. Clayton should have something to settle your stomach."

"I will," Shannon answered, hurrying away.

Jackie's eyes stayed on Mitch as the contest wore on. He seemed careless and indifferent, firing his arrows almost without aim. After the tournament, she was going to have to speak to him. There was no way of getting around it. She was going to have to make him believe that she knew nothing about the stolen jewelry. He was the only one who could help her find out who did.

Dave Kiernan won the archery contest and was rewarded by a kiss from his bride while everyone else applauded.

A table had been set up near the ladies and after the first of the contests, everyone went over to partake of cold beverages and sliced fruit. Jackie stayed talking with Maggi and a couple of the other ladies while she drank some punch. She stole a glance at Mitch and then became flushed when he caught her looking over at him. He gave her a cocky smile. She turned her head.

After the break for refreshments, the knights put on their helmets and mounted their horses for the jousting portion of the contest. It was just about impossible to pick out one knight from another. But Jackie had no trouble sighting Mitch. He'd transferred her headband to his arm, doubling it around his maille.

The first of the knights rode up to meet Paul—Paul being the opponent for each match. Jackie watched for a while, her attention going from the contest to Mitch, who was waiting on horseback for his turn.

"I think I should check on Shannon," Jackie said to Maggi as the knight before Mitch was defeated by Paul.

"I'm sure she's all right. Enjoy the contest." Maggi smiled, enjoying herself. "Oh, look," Maggi said. "Mitch is going to come up to you first."

"I'm going to look in on Shannon," Jackie said, getting to her feet. She didn't know what Mitch Corey had in mind, but she was sure she wasn't going to like it.

Mitch drew in on his reins, blocking Jackie's way. She had already started to walk. "Are you leaving, my lady?" he asked, taking off his helmet.

"I'm sure you will do me great honor even without my presence," Jackie said, managing to sound flippant.

"Go back to your seat," Mitch said with finality. "I want you where I can see you."

Jackie was just about to tell him off when there was a sudden commotion. The table with the refreshments went over, sending punch bowls, glasses, and platters of fruit clattering. A knight, on horseback nearby the table, yelled out through his visor for help.

Mitch jumped down from his horse. All the other knights rode up to the table—all, except for one. That knight rode straight up to Jackie. A gloved hand came down and tightened around her waist. The other gloved hand clamped over her mouth as the knight forcefully hoisted her up into his saddle.

Mitch was raising the table with a few of the other men when he caught a fast glimpse of the knight riding off with Jackie toward a section of woods at the side of the tournament field.

"Hey, what's going on?" Paul yelled, having taken in the same sight that Mitch had.

"Isn't this part of the fantasy?" Mitch asked, seeing a second knight ride off toward the woods.

"Not unless Jackie changed the script without telling me."

Mitch ran for his horse.

"Who are you? What is going on?" Jackie screamed as soon as the gloved hand was removed from her mouth.

"Ça ne fait rien . . ." the masculine voice behind the visor began to answer in perfect French. Changing to an accented English, the knight repeated, "It doesn't matter who I am."

"What is the meaning of this?" Jackie's voice was raised in alarm.

"Where is the jewelry, Mademoiselle?"

"What jewelry?" Jackie's heart skipped beats.

164

"Do not play dumb, Mademoiselle." The knight brought the stallion to a halt and waited for the second knight to catch up.

Jackie tried to pull off the knight's helmet, only to have her wrists clasped painfully.

"Does your lover have the jewelry?" The knight kept a hold of her wrists while also digging his elbow into her stomach.

"Yes," Jackie gasped as the pressure applied to her midsection threatened to cause her to retch.

"What do you want to do now?" the knight yelled.

It took Jackie a second to realize he wasn't addressing her, but was addressing the knight on the other horse. If the other knight answered, Jackie didn't hear him. What she heard was the hoofs of a third horse coming close.

She was riding again, the knight having kicked the stallion into a racing pace. Jackie looked back and saw Mitch riding hard toward them. Then Jackie saw something else. The knight holding her had pulled a gun out from his boot. Jackie screamed.

Mitch had caught up to the other knight and was just about to tackle him when a bullet whizzed by his shoulder. Still, Mitch managed a swing and with an ease that surprised him, Mitch quickly unseated the knight. The knight stayed down on the ground.

"Mitch . . . Mitch, go back," Jackie shouted, panicky. "Please, go back. Please, go ba . . ." She didn't finish. A maille-gloved hand socked her jaw and knocked her out.

Mitch brought his horse up short after the knight holding Jackie had done the same. Mitch saw Jackie being dropped down to the ground, her body limp. He slid down quickly from his horse, running to her and then everything went black. The knight had tossed his gun and caught Mitch at the side of his head.

Jackie came to first. Disoriented, her face hurting, it took Jackie a while to sit up. When she did, she saw Mitch sprawled out a few feet away from her. Breath sobbing in her throat, Jackie crawled to him.

"Mitch," Jackie screamed, touching his face with shaky fingers. Calling his name over and over again, she cradled his head in her lap and cried.

Mitch regained consciousness ten minutes later. He heard Jackie calling to him as he slowly opened his eyes. "Baby . . . you okay?" Mitch asked unsteadily.

"Mitch," Jackie whimpered, the tears still coming.

"Shh," Mitch said soothingly. With a gloved hand, he commanded the back of her neck and brought her head down to kiss her.

"Did you faint, baby?" Mitch asked softly, sitting up.

"He hit me," Jackie said dismissively. Her concern was with him. "Mitch, are you all right?"

"Where did he hit you?" Mitch exploded.

"My face," Jackie answered quickly. "Are you okay?"

Mitch yanked off his maille gloves. "I'm all right," he said, gingerly touching Jackie's face.

"It hurts when you touch." Jackie's eyes teared some more.

"Baby, do you know who it was?" Mitch stroked her shoulders and her arms with unsteady hands.

Jackie shook her head. "He wanted the jewelry and he knows that you have it." Jackie trembled as she spoke. "He's French . . . He spoke a few words of

166

French and he had an accent. It's got to be one of the guests . . . Two of the guests, I mean. But none of the guests are French." She rambled on.

"Oh, baby, I'm so sorry that I didn't believe you." Mitch caressed her hair. "Can you forgive me?"

"Yes, Mitch," Jackie whispered.

"We should get back to the castle. I want to get an icepack on your face. Baby, do you think you can ride with me?" Mitch could see that his stallion was close by.

"I can ride but what if you have a concussion? I don't think that you should ride."

"I don't have a concussion." Mitch rolled to his feet. He made sure he had his balance before he reached down to help Jackie stand. He'd had sufficient experience with concussions to know if he had one.

Just about everyone was gathered in the great hall when Jackie and Mitch walked into the castle.

"Honey, are you all right?" Maggi asked nervously, fluttering around Jackie.

"Yes, I'm fine," Jackie assured her.

"What the hell happened?" Paul questioned, looking from Jackie to Mitch.

"We all thought this was part of the fantasy," Joan Kiernan said, excitedly.

Dave Kiernan put an arm around his wife. "Is there something dangerous going on here that we should know about?"

Jackie gave Mitch a look that he thankfully interpreted. "There's nothing for anyone to be concerned about." Mitch smiled, trying to put everyone at ease. "It was just a surprise stunt that went haywire. Jackie

167

hired a couple of guys from St. Mary's to play it out and they got a little carried away."

"Why didn't you tell me you were going to do something like that?" Paul asked, showing Jackie that he was annoyed.

"What's the big deal?" Josh asked, his question going to Paul, which in turn caused an argument between the two men.

Mitch went over to Clayton and took him aside. "I'm going to need a couple of icepacks. Do you think you can help me out?"

"I just cracked a chunk of ice for Shannon not too long ago. There's plenty left. I'll throw some in two towels."

"What did Shannon need ice for?" Mitch realized as he looked around the hall that Shannon Grant was the only member of Camelot who was missing.

"Josh said that she had a headache and that she thought an icepack would make her feel better."

"Really," Mitch commented. The mind of the private investigator started to click in between the beats of a still throbbing head. "I'm going to take Jackie to her room. Do me a favor and send Nina up with the ice when you have it ready. Oh, and tell her to be inconspicuous about it."

Clayton shot Mitch a suspicious look. "What really happened?"

"Exactly what I said happened," Mitch answered.

Paul was just walking away from Jackie as Mitch came over to her. "Paul is going to try and get everyone down to the beach," Jackie said.

"Will Josh be joining Paul?" Mitch asked.

"I would guess so," Jackie answered. "I told Paul

that I was going to be helping Clayton in the kitchen and that you wouldn't be joining them. I said that you had fallen off your horse and that you were feeling some aches and pains."

"I'm sure Paul got a small thrill out of you telling him that I had taken some lumps." Mitch gave Jackie a wink and then he took her hand. "Let's get upstairs. Nina is going to bring up a couple of icepacks to your chamber."

"Your head is hurting, isn't it?" Jackie looked at Mitch tensely as they left the hall.

"You know me, I've got a hard head." Mitch smiled, climbing the stairs with her.

"Mitch, do you have any idea who it might be? I'm really scared."

"Don't be afraid, baby," Mitch said gently as they reached the top of the stairs. "Come with me into my chamber first so that I can get a change of clothes. I want to get out of this tin can."

In her chamber, Jackie helped Mitch out of his armor. Mitch put on a shirt and jeans. He was just zippering up when Nina knocked.

Nina came in with a bottle of champagne resting in a large bucket of ice, two cocktail glasses, and two white cotton towels.

"Please return my compliments to the chef," Mitch said, smiling at Clayton's ingenuity and appreciating the champagne.

After Nina closed the door, Jackie held the two glasses out. Mitch popped the champagne cork. "Did I ever tell you that I like the glow you get from champagne?"

"When did you see me glow from champagne?"

Jackie asked, smiling as best she could with her face feeling as if it had doubled in size.

"The night you came to the club." Mitch filled both of the glasses.

"I have a confession to make." Jackie's eyes were a bit bedeviled as she took a sip of her champagne.

"What confession is that?"

"Do you remember how I promised you that I wouldn't leave while you were playing your saxophone?"

Mitch nodded his head.

"I was going to leave before you got back to the table."

"What made you change your mind?"

"You looked so outrageously sexy playing your saxophone that I was sure if I tried to stand, I would swoon."

Mitch gave her an outrageously sexy smile. "And here I am without my horn."

"You don't need it," Jackie teased and then stifled a sudden yawn. "You are absolutely the sexiest man I have ever seen and I want you—and I love you." And she was swaying a little as champagne combined with shock and exhaustion.

Mitch grinned. "How about we both lie down on the bed with a couple of icepacks and this bottle of champagne and see what happens?" He knew she was going to be out like a light as soon as her head touched down.

"Okay," Jackie murmured, letting his arm at her waist guide her over to the bed.

She was sound asleep in less than three minutes. Mitch put some ice in a towel and placed it on her jaw, securing it there with the pillow that he wasn't going to be using. He kissed her forehead, whisking her hair gently aside and then he tiptoed out of the room.

Mitch knew exactly where he was heading. He knew who was fencing the jewels.

CHAPTER TEN

Mitch made his way down the stone hallway, circling around the parapet to the east wing. He stopped outside of Shannon Grant's chamber. He tried the knob while digging into his jeans pocket for the set of passkeys that he never left home without. As it turned out a key wasn't necessary. The door opened at the turn of the knob.

Shannon was lying down on her bed. Josh was sitting next to her holding a makeshift icepack on her forehead. He'd had his back to the door but he'd turned quickly as Mitch entered.

"I could have sworn you told me that you had no interest in Shannon," Mitch said casually. "And here you are playing doctor."

"What do you mean by just walking in here?" Josh snapped. "What the hell do you want?"

"It's the first time I ever hit a lady. My conscience was giving me some grief," Mitch answered easily. "How are you feeling, Shannon?"

Shannon sprang up, taking the towel that was tied to hold the ice from Josh. She dropped the icepack to the floor, started to say something but nothing came out. All she managed to do was look unstrung.

Mitch took a rush chair from the corner of the room and brought it up close to the bed. He turned the chair around and straddled it. "You needn't look so trapped. I'm not out to turn the two of you in. I'm here to make a deal. I have the jewelry. You have the buyer. I'd like to make a quick sale. You set it up for me and I give you a cut of the take. Nice and simple."

"What the hell are you talking about? What jewelry? What do you mean turn the two of us in? Turn us in for what?" Josh questioned, stealing a sideways glance at Shannon, who was recovering some of her composure.

Mitch ignored Josh's questions, including the one that followed about who the hell was he anyway. They both knew exactly who he was as well as knowing exactly what he was talking about. It wasn't hard to figure now that it was Shannon who had gone through his things under the guise of cleaning his room.

"If you two want to powwow for a second, I can turn my back. But—" Mitch paused significantly. "A second is all you've got. If you keep me hanging too long, I might just settle for the commission the insurance companies are willing to pay me for recovering the jewelry. Of course, if I do it that way, then I might just as well turn the two of you in."

"You've got nothing on us," Josh stated.

"Haven't I?" He didn't—at least nothing that a DA would pat him on the back for. All he really had was the hope that greed would win out over common sense.

"If you hadn't gotten nervous and planted the jewelry in Jackie's room, he wouldn't have anything," Shannon told Josh disgustedly.

"Shut up, Shannon," Josh retorted, aggravated.

"Do we deal or don't we?" Mitch inquired.

Neither Shannon nor Josh answered, though they did exchange a meaningful look between them. The meaning was easy enough for Mitch to decipher. Shannon was willing. Josh was not.

"Look, I don't want to have to give up a bonanza like this. Fast, easy money and I get along real nice. But if you don't want to tell me who's buying, then we're all going to come out losers. I don't want to chance holding on to the stuff for long."

"How much of a cut were you planning to give us?" Shannon asked, pointing to herself as the greedier of the two.

"Ten percent of the selling price," Mitch answered calmly, lowballing to open negotiations.

"Ten percent . . . That's ridiculous!" Shannon exclaimed.

Mitch stared straight at Josh, expecting Josh to quiet Shannon down. Instead, Josh stayed quiet himself, chewing something over in his head.

"What did you have in mind?" Mitch asked, directing the question to Shannon while his eyes stayed on Josh.

"We want half—fifty percent," Josh entered in, his face completely expressionless.

A flag came up—a bright red warning one. Josh was giving in too easy now. Did he have a hidden card up his sleeve? "How about I cut through the banter?" Mitch suggested, his features even. "I'll settle at forty percent for you and sixty percent for me."

"Are you going to be cutting Jackie in on your end?" Josh asked coolly.

"No, she's out of this. As far as she's concerned, I'm going to be turning the stuff over to the insurance companies. She doesn't know anything about your involvement. In fact, she still thinks that I suspect her, since I found the jewelry in her room. Of course, she also knows that I've decided to let her off the hook."

"Are you sure that she doesn't have any idea of your plans?" Josh asked.

"I don't share when I don't have to," Mitch answered lazily.

"Jackie is a problem. It's going to be hard keeping her in the dark," Josh pointed out.

"Why is that?" Mitch felt his nerves become raw just trying to anticipate why Josh saw Jackie as a problem. It was one thing for him to stick his neck out but he wasn't going to chance her beautiful neck as well.

"Well, you see we don't complete the deal until after she goes back with the rest of the tour. She expects Shannon and me to stay behind to pack up. What are you going to tell her to get out of going back with the others?"

So that was all there was to it . . . Relieved on that score, Mitch put his mind through some quick paces. "She won't suspect anything. I'll just tell her that I'm going to stay behind to turn the stuff over to the authorities here for return to the States. I'll tell her I'm nervous about carrying it back on my own."

"I suppose she'll buy that," Josh agreed.

"Then we have a deal?" Mitch asked.

"We have a deal," Josh answered, knowing Mitch Corey was not going to be happy with the deal he had in mind.

"Josh and Shannon . . . I still can't believe it," Jackie said, following Mitch into his apartment. He'd called her from the airport and asked her to meet him here. She'd been back in LA for two days now without him. A detective had come by the agency that morning to inform her about Shannon and Josh and how Mitch had been responsible for breaking the fencing operation. The detective had mentioned that there had been some trouble. He'd said something about guns and shooting but that no one had been hurt. Jackie had never felt so scared in all her life and she hadn't felt reassured until she'd heard Mitch's voice and then seen him.

Mitch dropped his suitcase and then led Jackie over to his blue corduroy sofa. "Josh was only a lackey. He made the deliveries and brought home the cash. There are some big boys behind him. I got enough names to keep the police busy for quite a while." He sat down and drew her down beside him.

"I hope you know that I am furious with you," Jackie said, not sounding at all angry. "You lied to me. When you told me to call the authorities from Penzance to meet you at the castle the next day just to turn over the jewelry, you already knew you were going to set a trap for Shannon and Josh. If I had known what you had in mind to do, I would never have left you."

Mitch grinned. "I know, that's why I lied to you." He strung himself out on the cushions, his legs outstretched, his head low against the sofa back. He was pretty exhausted but not that exhausted that his fingers didn't find their way to the pins keeping her hair in a twisted knot at the nape of her neck.

"Where did Shannon come into it? She first met Josh on this tour." Jackie sat primly with her long legs crossed at her ankles and her hands in the lap of her gently flared gray linen dress. She wanted to tell him not to take the knot of her hair apart. Do you know how much I love you? she wanted to cry. Don't you realize how many times I imagined the fantasy being real? You're my knight in shining armor. Only I know it's an illusion. I know that what you feel for me isn't going to last.

"They didn't just meet. Josh met Shannon six months ago. He fell in love with her and before long he'd told her what he was involved in and how in a few years, with the way things were going, he would have some real nice money stashed away. Shannon talked him into shortening the process. She wanted some real nice money right away and she came up with a plan." Mitch tossed the pins he was taking out of Jackie's hair, aiming for the steamer trunk in front of the sofa. Most of them landed on the floor.

"What was her plan?"

"I'll tell you but first I want to know if you missed me."

"I missed you," Jackie said, her voice catching along with her breath.

"How much?" Mitch asked, running his fingers through her loose hair. He was aware that there was something bothering her—she was setting up some kind of wall between them. He had been aware of it from the instant he'd arrived.

"I missed you very much," Jackie answered hoarsely.

"You pulled away from me downstairs." He tried not to let her see how worried that had him.

"There were people looking at us." Jackie offered him an excuse.

"There's no one looking at us now." He touched the corners of her mouth with his thumb. "Show me that you've missed me."

She thought about it. How much more would it hurt her later if she pretended the fantasy for a little longer?

"Please, baby. Show me."

Jackie slanted her head to his shoulder and moved her hands inside his white cotton blazer jacket. Her palms traveled across his blue polo shirt and she felt the heat of his hard body. Her own temperature was rising by double degrees.

Mitch opened his mouth to her but he let her control the kiss and she kept it soft and sweet.

"I missed you, baby," Mitch murmured against her lips.

She moved away from him on the couch. "Tell about Shannon?" she asked, speaking after she'd swallowed hard.

Mitch jammed his hands in the pockets of his white slacks and rested his head. He tried talking himself out of worrying. He wasn't going to lose her. He couldn't lose her.

"I'm not going to tell you anything if you don't come closer."

It wasn't an ultimatum, but a plea. Jackie slid back to his side. "Now tell me."

He looked up at her with his head still against the cushion. He tried reading her green eyes but he wasn't able to. "Shannon talked Josh into making this delivery for themselves. They were going to pocket the cash and take off for France. Shannon and Josh had a place all ready and waiting for them in Paris. They had been making their plans for the past couple of months— getting set for this tour." Mitch talked but that wasn't what he wanted to do. He wanted her in his arms. He wanted to be back with her where they had been.

"But how did they know then that Shannon would be on the tour?"

"Shannon had Josh bribe the woman who usually came with you. He gave her five thousand dollars to get sick. Shannon volunteered then, crossing her fingers that you would take her. Josh had wanted her to just go to Paris and wait for him but she was afraid that Josh would back out without her there to egg him on. Shannon had his number."

"How did you figure out that it was Shannon and Josh? When did you figure it out?" Jackie fought hard not to smooth the wave of hair that had fallen low on his forehead.

"I figured it out when we got back after those two knights rode off with you. It was something Clayton said that tipped me off. I had taken him aside and asked him to make up two icepacks for us. He said that Josh had already asked him for an icepack for Shannon. Josh had told Clayton that Shannon had a headache. I knew that I had knocked one of the knights off his horse. It came to me that I had done so without any trouble at all. And so I deduced that one of the two knights was probably not a knight."

179

"The second knight was Shannon Grant," Jackie affirmed. "When she told me she was leaving the tournament because she wasn't feeling well, it was an excuse not to be missed."

"Right," Mitch said.

"And I wouldn't have thought anything about Josh's absence because he always left after the archery contest to get ready for the evening's entertainment."

"Shannon and Josh both put on suits of armor and rode onto the field. Shannon turned the table over to distract my attention from you."

"Why did they put the jewelry in my room?"

"Not they . . . Josh put the jewelry in your room because he knew who I was and he got cold feet. He wanted out of the whole operation and he figured if I did find the jewelry, I would hang it on you. As I did," Mitch added, looking at her softly.

"How did Josh find out who you were?" Jackie asked. The tenderness in his blue gaze set off a wave of longing.

"Josh was suspicious of me right from the start. I guess I didn't fit the profile of your usual tour customer. Shannon searched through my things. It took her a few times but she finally found my license. I should have realized something was up when I caught her in my room late one day. Only my head was filled with thoughts of an enchantress with honey-blond hair and green eyes." Mitch took one hand from the pocket of his slacks and touched that honey-blond hair.

"Please, Mitch," Jackie whispered uncomfortably. "I want to hear the whole story."

Mitch took his fingers out of her hair. "There isn't much more to it," he said, releasing a long-drawn-out sigh. "When Josh told Shannon that he planted the jewels on you, she got furious. She went to your chamber that night during dinner to retrieve them but I had already taken them. She checked my room afterward without any luck."

"What had you done with the jewelry?"

"I took the box down to that lake you like, dug a hole and hid it. Josh took you from the tournament just to find out for sure which one of us had the jewels."

"Oh, I see," Jackie said. "When did you let on to Shannon and Josh that you knew it was them?"

"After the champagne put you out, I went to them and told them that I was looking to deal. I offered to split with them if they would set me up with their contact." He decided not to tell her that Josh had tried double-dealing him, though she'd probably find out during the trial.

"Was the contact one of the guests?"

"No," Mitch answered. "Josh hooked up with his contact at the end of the tour, after you left. He had contacts at each of your tour locations—people who were more than happy to get a deal on stolen jewelry from the States."

Jackie stared ahead thoughtfully. "Josh always stayed behind a day or two to get all the props packed. And, of course, I didn't think anything of Shannon staying with him because he needed help."

Mitch raised himself and leaned in front of her, intending to kiss her. Instead, he wound up just studying her face intently. "Are you going to marry me, Jackie?" he asked quietly.

"I'm afraid to even think about it." She spoke so

low that he might not have heard her if he hadn't been so close.

"Why are you afraid?"

"Because I'm so much in love with you."

"I'm even more in love with you. I'm bigger than you are," Mitch said, teasing to lighten the intensity.

"How do I know that you'll always love me? How do I know we can make it married?"

"You know because I say we can. I promise you that we can."

"Do you always keep your promises?"

"Always."

"I'd rather we just stay lovers. I'd rather we just stay the way we are."

"It isn't enough. I want you to make a lifelong commitment to me and I want you to trust that I'm making the same commitment to you. I won't settle for less than that."

"What do you mean you won't settle for less than that?"

"You know what I mean."

"I'm not sure that I do. Are you saying that you would end what we have now?"

"Jackie, if we try to stay the way you want us to stay, it will end itself. Can't you see that?"

"No, I can't. All I want is to just feel safe."

Mitch leaned his head back against the cushion. "Jackie, love means being willing to take risks. I can't say to you that it's all going to be smooth sailing. I'm sure there will be some rough spots but we'll work them out together. The most important thing is trusting each other."

"Trusting is hard to do."

"Maybe you're just not as much in love with me as you say you are. Maybe we should just split up for a while so that you can have some time to think. I don't want to get what I want by pressuring you."

She gazed at him searchingly, knowing that the thing she feared the most was happening and she was powerless to stop it. She tried to tell herself that it was better that it was over between them now than later. But she didn't feel better about it at all. "I do love you, Mitch," she said, holding back the tears that misted her eyes.

Jackie picked up her handbag and then got to her feet. "Will you call me?" she asked, pretending that there was still some hope.

"Sure, I'll call you in a few days."

He didn't call.

Jackie hadn't expected he would. But it didn't stop her from praying that he'd be on the other end of the line every time her phone rang. It didn't stop her from hoping desperately that he'd be waiting for her one day when she walked out of the agency. It didn't stop her from feeling more miserable as each day blended into another and then another . . .

Two weeks later, Jackie sat down at her desk and called his office. She didn't know what she was going to say to him but she knew if she didn't at least hear his voice she was going to go crazy.

Mitch's secretary, Carly O'Neill, picked up the phone.

"Is Mr. Corey in?" Jackie asked, her heart racing.

"He's out for the day," Carly answered. "Who's calling?"

183

Disappointment running rampant, Jackie's heart sank. "This is Jacqueline Lacey. Could you tell him that I called." Could you tell him to please call me, she wanted to say, but didn't.

"Just a minute," Carly said rapidly, catching Jackie before she hung up. "I hope you've got something to tell him that he wants to hear. I'd like to see him rejoin the human race."

"Has he told you about me?" Jackie asked, startled.

"Not directly." Carly grinned over the phone. "But he did get himself smashed. I found him in the office one morning mumbling into an empty bottle of Scotch. You've got to know that he's wild about you."

Her heart did flips. She loved him. He loved her. What more of a guarantee could she want than that . . . "If you speak to him before I do, could you tell him . . ." Jackie was interrupted by a knock on her door. "Hold on a minute," Jackie said to Carly as Fran Lumas, her new receptionist, stepped in.

"There's some guy outside who wants to see you," Fran said, smiling.

"Give me a minute and then send him in." Jackie brought the receiver back to her ear.

"He can't come in," Fran said, her smile broadening. "Besides, I don't think that you'd want him to come in at the moment."

Jackie said to Carly, "I'll call you back." She hung up and then came around her desk. "If there is someone giving you a hard time outside, call security."

"I think you should see him," Fran said, insisting.

Exasperated, Jackie sighed. She wanted to get back to the phone and find Mitch. Instead, she followed Fran out to the reception area.

"Where is he?" Jackie asked, looking around.

Fran jerked her thumb toward the outside door.

"You mean he's outside on the street?"

Fran nodded.

"Well, I guess you used your head not letting him in." Jackie thought once more of calling security to deal with the problem.

"He was in." Fran smiled. "But then he said he wanted to go back out to his horse."

"Horse?" Jackie asked, stopping after starting for the door.

"Horse," Fran confirmed. "This guy must be a real joker—not that I'd mind him joking around with me. Prepare yourself . . . He's also wearing a suit of armor."

"Did you say a suit of armor?" The question was left hanging in the air behind her. She was already flying out the door.

"Mitch!" Jackie shouted, fighting her way through a crowd of people who'd gathered around a knight in shining armor sitting on top of a white stallion.

"My lady," Mitch said, winking at her.

She was smiling. He was smiling. Everyone looking on was smiling.

"What are you doing?" Jackie asked, her eyes excited and happy.

"Come up here with me and I'll tell you." He kicked free of one stirrup and extended his hand. Jackie took a firm hold of his forearm. With ease, he set her up into the saddle with him.

"What are you up to?" she asked, touching his armor, touching his face.

"I got to thinking that in days of old the knights

were bold and so I'm not asking you to marry me anymore, I'm telling you that you're going to marry me."

"When?" Jackie cried, happy tears somersaulting down her face.

"Hey, are they making a movie here?" someone in the crowd asked.

"They must be," came an answer.

"Don't cry, baby. Please," Mitch begged, then asked with underscored anxiety, "When? Do you mean that you will marry me?"

"Yes, Mitch, yes."

"Oh, baby . . ."

"Are you sure we're going to make it?"

"I'm positive." Mitch grinned. "I'm always going to be your knight in shining armor and you are always going to be my enchantress."

"Could you kiss me now," Jackie whispered. "I need just a little more assurance. No . . . Actually, I don't need any more assurance. I just want to be kissed."

Mitch teased. "I thought you didn't like me kissing you with anyone looking on."

"I don't see anyone," Jackie murmured.

Smiling, Mitch bent his head and gave his future wife what she wanted.

Neither the enchantress nor the knight paid any attention to the applause from the crowd.